Porcelain Doll

by

Joe Cosentino

A Jana Lane Mystery

Porcelain Doll

Cover Art by *Debbie Taylor*

The Wild Rose Press, Inc.
PO Box 708
Adams Basin, NY 14410-0708
Visit us at www.thewildrosepress.com

Publishing History
First Vintage Rose Edition, 2016
Print ISBN 978-1-5092-0603-2
Digital ISBN 978-1-5092-0604-9

A Jana Lane Mystery
Published in the United States of America

Dedications

To Fred
for everything over all these years,
Melanie and the entire staff of The Wild Rose Press,
everyone who loves movies,
and the many readers who loved *PAPER DOLL*
and begged for another Jana Lane mystery.

Chapter 1

1982

Jana Lane, America's most famous ex-child star, ran on the grounds of her estate. The forty-year-old kept up a quick pace as someone, or something, followed closely in the woods just out of sight. Her heart pounded, and sweat dripped down her neck, arms, and legs. As she turned to avoid falling into the lake, Jana raced past a large oak tree. A hand reached out from a branch. Jana screamed.

Waking with a gasp, Jana rested her head on her silver satin pillow and took in some deep breaths. Then, she sat up in bed and tried to shake away the nightmare.

Keep it together, girl. Don't go off the deep end like before.

Thinking that music might help, she flipped on the radio, perched on her white and gold French provincial night table.

As Diana Ross crooned "Mirror Mirror," Jana rose then stood in front of her floor-length oval mirror. Staring back between the white and gold molding was a forty-year-old woman with porcelain skin, sky-blue eyes, a button nose, deep dimples, ruby red lips, and velvety strawberry-blonde hair. Yet, all Jana could focus on were her newly acquired crow's feet, laugh lines, frown lines, and three gray hairs. After giving birth to three children, the figure underneath her pink satin nightgown was still shapely and petite, but Jana only noticed the tiny belly and unwelcome stirrings of cellulite. Moving to the red satin canopy bed with its gold circular headboard, Jana slipped on her silver satin robe and fluffy pink slippers. Feeling a man's strong hands around her, she screamed.

Brian Otley, about the same age as Jana, had come out of their spa bathroom with a towel draped around his tiny waist, and embraced his wife.

Jana turned to watch droplets of water cascading from Brian's soft chestnut hair onto his perfectly sculpted shoulders, mountainous pectoral muscles, and six-pack abdominals.

Why is it that Brian seems to be living in flashback sequences, and I'm on fast forward?

His warm hazel eyes twinkled. "Sorry I scared you, babe."

Dropping her head Jana replied, "I can relate. I've been scaring myself lately, too."

Brian took his wife in his arms, pressed her closely into him, and they shared a warm, wet kiss. "What's up?"

Just ask your towel. "Since I turned forty, I guess I've been feeling a little…lost."

Brian released her, dropped the towel onto the Persian rug, and headed for their C.S. Lewis-style wardrobe. "I turned forty, and *I* don't feel any different."

Or look any different. "I had a nightmare. I was in our woods…running away from someone."

"Everybody has nightmares, babe."

"Especially me."

"Is it like before?" Brian asked with concern showing on his handsome face.

"No. These aren't memories." Moving to the silver-framed picture of Jana and her family on the white and gold armoire, Jana said, "Do you realize I haven't worked since I was eighteen years old?" Jana recalled leaving Hollywood after her breakdown when Brian put her back together like a toymaker mending a broken doll.

Standing in his briefs at their balcony door, looking like Zeus reigning over the heavens, Brian responded, "You did all that fundraising for the FDR estate, and aren't you planning something at the Vanderbilt mansion?" Brian turned to face her, and the sun rose over the mountains behind him, magically changing the sky from gray to azure. "And you take care of me and the kids."

And who takes care of me? Jana sat at her crushed velvet-trimmed vanity, and brushed her once-famous hair.

Brian disappeared into his walk-in closet. "I know things have been rough with your Guy Friday moving out to take care of his mom. But things will get easier when what's her name starts working for us."

If I hadn't been a household name throughout your childhood, I bet you'd forget my name, too. "Her name's Gloria Covetry. *You* recommended her."

"She interviewed for a job at Otley Architecture. Sweet kid."

A kid who is twenty-five, gorgeous, and transfixed by your every word. "Why didn't you hire her at your company?"

"She was woefully unqualified."

Jana frowned. "So, you hired her to work as our nanny?"

Brian peeked out at her. "Babe, is this about me having to travel?"

She put down the brush, and shrugged her pale shoulders. "I don't know what this is about. Maybe I'm having a mid-life crisis."

Brian exited the closet in a three-piece designer gray suit. Sitting on the gold-trimmed chaise, he put on his designer socks and Italian loafers.

Things have certainly changed since you wore faded jeans, a T-shirt, and a bandana for your landscaping jobs.

"Do you think it's menopause?"

Jana threw her brush at him, and they shared a laugh.

After lifting Jana to her feet, her husband gathered her into a comforting embrace and gazed at her with adoration in his soft eyes. "You know I'm nothing without you, babe. You and the kids are my whole world."

Brian smelled like the outdoors. After a lengthy hug and a lingering kiss, Jana felt more relaxed, but still unsettled.

He playfully slapped her behind. "Babe, I'm always here for you, whatever you need, whenever you need it. I'll always protect you from the nighttime boogie men."

She wrapped her hands around his thick, strong thumbs. It felt like home. "I love you, Brian." She meant it.

He kissed her nose. "You're the only girl for me." Then he put her down, disappeared again into his walk-in closet, and came out carrying his gym bag. "I'm going to the gym during lunch."

"What about breakfast?"

Brian replied, "I'll get something at work." After kissing her cheek, Brian added, "I may not be home until late. So don't wait dinner for me. I'll kiss the kids goodbye on the way out. Love you, babe." And he was gone.

Jana grasped the Jana Lane porcelain doll from the top of her dresser. She recalled posing for it when she was ten years old. She looked into the doll's clear blue eyes, stroked her long, blonde hair, and fluffed into place her pink velvet dress. *Everything else changes, but you.*

The moment Brian drove off in his red Italian sports car, Jana heard Devon, 10, and Ed, 8, scream in shrieking unison from down the hall, "Mom!" That in turn caused Brian Jr., 15 months, to wake with a piercing wail. Jana put her doll back on her dresser, took a deep breath, and headed down the hall to her children's bedrooms.

Two hours later, Jana had given the boys their breakfast. With Devon and Ed lost in a videogame battle in the playroom, Jana changed Brian Jr.'s diaper then put him inside his playpen next to her kitchen desk.

As she finished, Theresa arrived. The elderly housekeeper, wearing her black dress and white apron, complained about her sore feet as she wiped egg, spinach, and potato off the breakfast nook, two islands, and appliances. After she mopped the kitchen floor, Theresa sat at the marble island counter across from the television set, contemplating her upcoming soap opera.

"I think today will be the day Felicity finds out her father is really her brother, and her sister is really her mother." When the doorbell rang, Theresa rose slowly, rubbing her lower back.

Jana told Theresa to stay put and headed for the front hallway, where she opened the heavy door. Upon seeing her new nanny, she said, "Welcome, Gloria. Thank you for coming."

"Oh my goodness. This place is amazing!" Gloria Covetry's blue eyes doubled in size. "Mr. Otley said you had five acres of property, but I had no idea it was a palace!"

Jana blushed. "You are very sweet, Gloria."

"No, I'm not. I mean, I'm a sweet person…at least I hope I am, but this house is fantastic!" Standing in the entranceway, Gloria surveyed the cathedral ceiling, skylights, grandfather clock, window seat, aqua/gold/amber stained-glass window, prism chandelier, and saffron marble floor leading to the spiral stairs. "I feel like Cinderella at the ball."

I guess that makes me the Wicked Stepmother. "Please come in, Gloria."

"You don't have to ask me twice!"

A few minutes later, Jana and Gloria were seated in the all white front sitting room on high-backed, crushed velvet arm chairs flanking either side of the white marble fireplace mantel. Fitting into the furniture, Gloria wore a white blouse and navy blue skirt. A pearl necklace sculpted her smooth neck. Jana couldn't help but notice how much the blonde young woman resembled her.

When I was fifteen years younger. "Gloria, this is a live-in position. Are you okay with that?"

"Okay? Sure!"

"Brian showed me all the paperwork, and your references were fine."

"He is so nice." Gloria slid to the edge of her seat. "When I didn't get the secretarial job at the architecture firm, he felt so guilty; he asked me what other things I can do. When I told him my father died when I was ten years old, and I had to take care of my three brothers and sisters so my mother could work, he offered me the nanny job here. He said you've been...out of sorts lately." Blinking back tears, Gloria added, "Your husband has a big heart."

And a big mouth.

After serving Gloria tea from a sterling silver teapot, Jana said, "We should go over your duties."

Gloria took the china cup, enjoyed a sip, then placed it on a white end table. "Mr. Otley gave me Devon and Ed's schedules for school, karate, soccer, and swimming lessons." She took a pad out of her purse. "I've also got Brian Jr.'s nap, feeding, diaper, and play schedule. It seems your husband hasn't forgotten a thing, Mrs. Otley."

Except your name. "Please, call me, Jana. Where's your luggage, Gloria?"

"It's in my car. If you like, I can drop Devon and Ed off at school, then unpack."

"All right. Your room is the third door on the left upstairs. The children are dying to meet you, Gloria."

"And I can't wait to meet them. They looked so adorable in the pictures in Mr. Otley's office."

As Jana walked Gloria to the playroom, Gloria said, "My mother nearly had a heart attack when I told her I'd be working for you. But I have to admit, I've never seen any of your movies. I guess they were before my time."

"They're ancient history, I'm afraid." *Like me.*

"But while I'm here, I want to see every one of your movies on videotape."

Jana laughed. "We don't pay you enough for that."

Upon being introduced to their new nanny, Devon and Ed leapt from the beige sectional sofa opposite the home entertainment center, and jumped up and down like pogo sticks. "We like her, Mommy," shouted Devon. "She's pretty like you, only younger."

And why did I have children?

"Can I show Gloria the mole on my stomach?" asked Ed.

Gloria giggled. "We'll have lots of time to get to know each other, guys. Now it's off to school."

Jana kissed her sons then said to Gloria, "Thank you for helping us out, Gloria. Do you know how to get to Hyde Park Elementary?"

Gloria responded, "Sure. That's where *I* went."

"Perfect. Please drive carefully."

"I will."

After Jana waved goodbye to Gloria and the kids, she brought the tea things into the kitchen.

Theresa put them in the sink. "Gloria reminds me of Cassandra on my third soap opera. She stole Octavia's husband then had triplets. Three men think they're the father."

Jana replied, "Gloria has a lot of energy. And she relates well with the kids."

"From what I heard, it sounds like she relates well with Brian, too."

With Theresa watching Brian Jr. (the youngest

soap opera viewer), Jana went upstairs to her home gym. Clad in sweat clothes, she flipped on a cassette tape of Olivia Newton John singing "Physical" and hit the hand weights, slant board, and treadmill. Jana sweated, huffed, and puffed to the mirror, then headed back to her bedroom's walk-in closet. Since it was a warm June day, after changing from her sweat clothes into a one-piece aqua bathing suit with matching swim cape, Jana headed downstairs through the kitchen and out the French doors to her heart-shaped pool. Thanks to her childhood years in Hollywood starring in films like *The Surfer Girl*, Jana was a very strong swimmer and diver. She dove in and swam a few laps, then treaded water, taking in the gorgeous Hudson Valley, New York high-peaked mountains and glistening river in the distance.

After drying off with a terrycloth towel from the cabana, Jana went back into the house to her bedroom, and changed into a peach V-neck sweater and a skirt with a herringbone gold necklace. She teased then combed her hair until it sculpted her face and blanketed her shoulders. Finally, she applied peach-colored nail polish and lipstick.

Jana heard the doorbell and blew her nails dry. By the time she got downstairs, Theresa had let in Jana's guest. Knowing where to find him, Jana entered the music room, and noticed her visitor staring at the line of faded movie posters on the periwinkle wall.

"There never was and never will be a star as bright as you, Jana Lane. And I was the star-keeper." Simon Huckby, somewhere between sixty and a hundred years old, wore a chartreuse pants suit and lime shoes. The emaciated, small man wiped a tear off his wrinkled cheek with a rose-colored handkerchief. "When I discovered you in that play with your father in New York, I found gold. You were a rare treasure I protected, cultivated, polished, and displayed like the Crown Jewels."

Realizing nothing she could say or do would stop Simon's opening monologue, Jana stood and watched like an audience member at a matinee performance.

Touching a poster as if it were a deity, Simon said, "Jana Lane in *The Little Shop Girl*. You were the only child star with billing over the title. *I* got that for you. And you *deserved* it." After wiping the tears from his large brown eyes, Simon walked from poster to poster. "*Daddy's Girl, The Adorable Orphan, The Girl Detective, The Tiny Eskimo, Indian Princess, The Cowgirl and the Bandit, The Littlest Farmer, Jungle Girl, Little Girl on the Ranch, School Spy, Young Mermaid, Hawaiian Holiday, Pink Ballerina, The Pirate Princess, The Cutest Scientist, Surfer Girl, Going Ape, The Small Sailor, Girl Astronaut, The Sweet Candy Striper*. He stopped at the last poster displaying a picture of Jana on a horse as a girl sheriff in *Sugar and Spice*. "And then it all went away."

"Simon, it's so good to see you." Jane threw her arms around her old agent.

Careful not to mess her makeup, or his, Simon returned the hug. Then he stepped back to survey his mentee. "You look good enough to eat, baby doll."

"Let's sit down." Jana led Simon to a Prussian blue sofa next to a white baby grand piano surrounded by Degas paintings.

"This is Cornelius' favorite room," Simon said, as he accepted tea and cookies on a delicate china plate.

"You know musicians."

Jana asked, "How are things going with you two?"

"Fine for now." Placing a royal-blue silk napkin on his tiny knee, Simon said, "I don't mean to sound like Dolly Levy, but after so many years with Mr. Right, and countless years alone after Jonas died, I'm not thinking about tomorrow." Voraciously digging into an almond cookie, he added, "Who ever thought I'd be with a cello-playing, motorcycle-riding, nearly seven-foot-tall senior citizen?"

Between sips of her tea, Jana said, "How long will you be staying with Cornelius in Rhinebeck?"

"For a while." Simon winked. "Did I mention Cornelius plays the tuba, too?"

They shared a laugh.

"I'm finally selling my old relic of a house in LA."

Jana did a double-take. "Are you giving up show business?"

Simon waved a small hand at her. "Show business gave up on me…after you left me."

It took two minutes longer than usual for the guilt trip.

"Cornelius said I can stay with him as long as I like. It's a big house for only one person." Simon giggled. "And he has the hots for me…big time."

They shared another laugh.

"Enough about me." Simon put his china cup and saucer down on a Louis XIV side table. "What's wrong, doll?"

Jana did the same. "Nothing. I'm fine."

Scratching the dyed red hair encircling his bald pate, Simon said, "Baby doll, you never had a false moment on screen." He took her hand in his. "And you kept nothing from me then. Please, don't start now."

It will probably help to get it off my chest.

Collapsing back onto the sofa, Jana said, "Two years ago, after I figured out what happened to me back in Hollywood during *Sugar and Spice*, I felt exonerated, free, and dare I say, happy."

"But?"

"But in the process, I lost my family, my friends, nearly everyone in my life."

Simon cleared his throat.

Jana squeezed his little knee. "I know I'll always have you, Simon."

"You bet your SAG card." He sipped his tea. "You still play tennis at your club?"

"With strangers *now*."

"And you are the only celebrity doing fundraising for AIDS. Everybody else is afraid to touch it."

"I'm far from being a celebrity anymore, Simon."

Looking up at the gold-framed portrait of Jana and Brian, Simon said, "What about hubby and the kids?"

"I am incredibly blessed to have such a wonderful family, but Devon and Ed are busy with their activities. They'll be going away to summer camp soon. Brian Jr. is still a toddler."

"And Brian Sr.?"

"Now that his architecture firm has taken off, Brian's been traveling more frequently than a pilot."

"And you aren't up for being a stewardess?"

Jana looked at Simon incredulously. "I love my husband dearly. But two years ago, I learned I need more in my life than being Brian's wife." She avoided his eyes. "And I've been having nightmares again."

"What kind of nightmares?"

"Somebody chases me through our woods."

He took her hand. "You went through a lot, baby doll. It might take a little more time to work things through." Simon grinned. "Or maybe you're psychic, and your dream is a premonition of an upcoming film, where you play *Jane of the Jungle*."

"I don't think so, Simon." Jana scanned the framed posters on the wall. "That little girl who scaled mountains to see her grandpa, darted away from robbers on horseback, healed the sick, captured thugs, rescued captives in quicksand, slid across glaciers to save a ship, tamed a giant wave to protect a group of surfers, and won the hearts of everyone in America, feels as worn out, lined, and yellowed as those old posters."

"I agree."

"Gee, Simon, if you've lost faith in me, I might as well pack it in."

"Quite the opposite, baby girl." Simon rubbed his small hands together as if he was making a campfire. "*You* are going back on the silver screen."

Groaning like a teenager with a late allowance, Jana replied, "We've already gone down that rocky road, and we got lost in the maze."

"*This* is different." Simon adjusted the cantaloupe scarf around his neck. "I received a totally unsolicited call from a producer at Caeneus Films, and they want *you* as the lead of their next picture."

Jana responded, "And you were totally surprised by this *unsolicited call*?"

"I may have put out some feelers around town, but Caeneus was the first to bite." He added with a diabolical look, "And I reeled them in like a twenty-pounder."

Jana raised her eyes to the crystal chandelier. "Simon, I'm too old. Nobody wants to see my movies anymore."

Simon clutched at his chest as if he had been stabbed with a dagger. "Our public hasn't forgotten! Jana Lane paper dolls still sell."

In nursing homes.

"And you're only forty years old. You haven't even ripened yet. I've got...a certain number of years over you, and I'm still hot...or cool...or tepid...or whatever the young people say nowadays." Simon moved his scarf over a hickey mark on his neck. "Just ask Cornelius."

"How do they...how do *we* know I can still act?"

"I sent Myrna Buller a videotape of you on public television soliciting donations for AIDS research." He added with an acrimonious sneer, "The mayor, the governor, and the president can pretend AIDS doesn't exist, but Jana Lane will once again save the day."

"They cast me in a movie based on *that*? And who's Myrna Buller?"

"Studios no longer sign actors to long term contracts. And believe me, I got you the best contract years ago. Nowadays, mega managers create package deals with their clients as screenwriter, director, and stars then pitch it to the movie companies. Myrna was a gymnast in her youth who married then divorced a movie producer. Now a top theatrical manager, she uses the discipline, determination, and grit she had as a gymnast to get work for her only A-list clients."

Laughing, Jana replied, "I think I'm on the Z-list."

"Not for long." Simon added with a huge grin, "I

told Myrna about your interest in making a comeback film—"

"*My* interest?"

"—And she was intrigued. After we had a power lunch at the Brown Derby, Myrna got to work and created a package with her clients and *you*. She approached the people at Caeneus Films like a rabid dog and they bit."

"Who are her clients?"

"Jack Capello will direct."

"Didn't he direct that big thriller last year?"

Simon nodded like a woodpecker. "And the big news is your leading man will be...Jason Apollo!"

Jana's jaw dropped. "The big heartthrob?"

"None other. And I negotiated equal billing, a nine-figure salary, and profit sharing including foreign distribution and toys in exchange for your agreement to promote the film upon release as your big comeback."

Why do I feel like I'm sinking down instead of coming back?

"Myrna also has Tom Strong, a well respected macho man supporting actor, and Trevor Masquer, a brooding young method actor for the film."

Jana realized she had stopped breathing. Sucking in air, she said, "Simon, I appreciate the offer, but this isn't a good time."

"I agree. This is the *perfect* time." He flailed his thin arms. "How long can you mope around here alone like Greta Garbo?"

"Simon, I—"

"Now shush, baby doll, and hear me out."

Jana sat up straight, pressed her knees together, and listened attentively like a scolded child in grade school.

Simon said, "Baby girl, my purpose, my goal, and my desire in life have always been to serve you, protect you, and honor your talents. Hasn't it?"

And make ten percent of the proceeds. "Simon, I have a toddler and two small children. I can't traipse off to Hollywood to fling my body in front of a green screen as *E.T.'s* mom or whoever else is in vogue."

As Jana had seen him do so many times before, Simon tugged at the diaper underneath his pants suit. "That's why this is perfect."

"The only way it would be perfect is if the film were shooting in my house."

Simon smiled like a jack-o-lantern.

Jana shot up like fireworks. "This house? *My* house! They want to shoot the film *here*?"

Nodding proudly, Simon said, "I inadvertently showed Myrna pictures of the house, and she showed the director of photography and cinematographer who shared them with the film's producers. They're paying us a hefty fee to use your estate."

"Simon—"

With the success of films like *Ordinary People* and *On Golden Pond*, the studios want to shoot more films on location."

"But why *this* location?"

"Because it's the *ideal l*ocation." Simon pulled her back down onto the sofa. "You've heard about John Hinckley shooting at the President to impress Jodie Foster?"

"Who hasn't?"

Simon leaned forward, and added in a whisper, "From what I hear, Hinckley was wasting his time."

Jana's eyes narrowed. "You think everyone is gay,

Simon."

Simon mocked offense. "Not *everyone*. Just all the people in Hollywood." He ran a finger over a tweezed eyebrow. "Anyway, with Hinkley such a big story, the movie studios are chomping at the slate board to cash in on Reagan's and Jodie's misfortunes—who are both actors by the way."

Throwing her hands up in the air, Jana asked, "But what does this have to do with *me?*"

Placing his napkin on the side table, Simon said, "The movie, your comeback film, is about an ex-child star, played by you, who is married and living in Hyde Park, New York. She—you—hire a young man, played by Trevor Masquer, as your personal assistant who falls in love with you. When you rebuke him, he assassinates your husband, the governor, played by Tom Strong, to get your attention. After you turn him down, Trevor plots to kill you. But you are saved by the handsome and virile detective, the incredibly sexy Jason Apollo of course, who falls under your spell." Simon's face lit up like a store window. "So, what do you think?"

Jana laughed. "It's a far cry from *The Girl Detective.*"

"Brian will be out of town on business. The boys will be away at summer camp. Theresa can take care of Brian Jr. during commercial breaks."

"I just hired a new nanny."

"Perfect. Besides, you'll be living and working right here on your estate, so you can check in on Brian Jr. every time he dribbles on his bib or poops in his diaper."

"Simon, I won't allow a film crew to tromp around and destroy my home."

Putting his small arm around her, Simon said, "Baby girl, they will move around here like soldiers tiptoeing through a mine field. You have my word."

Jana's head was reeling. "When do they want to start shooting?"

Simon opened a miniscule pouch at his waist, put on the gold-rimmed glasses attached to the chain around his neck, and examined a sheet of paper. "Meetings, fittings, camera tests, and rehearsals start the end of the month. Shooting the week after."

"It starts shooting in less than a month!"

"They don't want another studio to beat them to it. Besides, you just said you have nothing to do, and nobody to do it with. And you were having nightmares." He crowed like Peter Pan. "So I just solved your problems." He winked at her. "Admit it, baby girl. You want to do this."

I feel like I'm on a roller coaster careening off the track. "I haven't even read the script."

Simon jumped up like a jack-in-the-box, and pointed like a game show model to a large envelope on Jana's Louis XIV desk. "So read. What other problems do you need me to solve, doll?"

Joining him at the desk, Jana replied, "Deciding if I want to do it."

"You want to do it."

"And telling Brian."

"I'll tell him."

Jana looked at their picture. "Thanks, Simon, but I'll need to do that all by myself."

After Simon left, Jana sat in a hanging white wicker swing on her glass sun porch, and read the script of *His Obsession* like a drug addict getting a fix. When she finished the last page, Jana rested back on the bougainvillea print cushion.

It's rare that a film script has such strong character development, captivating plot, intelligent dialogue, and interesting subtext. Jack Capello is a good director. Tom Strong is a fine actor. And Jason Apollo is...Jason Apollo. Could doing the film get me out of this state of depression?

Jana jumped off the swing, just escaping the Tiffany chandelier above and the glider nearby. She was surprised to hear herself say, "I'm doing this!"

Chapter 2

That evening, Jana sat in her dining room at the head of her long maple table with a baby intercom in case Brian Jr. woke in his bedroom upstairs. Gloria sat opposite Jana in front of the maple and glass china cabinet. Devon and Ed were between them on either side, twirling their silver napkin holders and throwing pieces of chicken with polenta and truffled mushrooms (a dish served on one of Theresa's soap operas) at the purple peacocks on the wallpaper.

"Hey, this isn't boot camp, guys. Sit like gentlemen and eat your dinner, please," Gloria said calmly.

"Sure, Gloria."

"Sorry, Gloria."

To Jana's surprise, the boys behaved like little soldiers. *Why didn't I hire a nanny years ago?*

"I got an A on a math test today, Mom," Devon said between bites of his polenta.

Gloria said through the silver candleholders, "Don't talk with your mouth full, Dev."

Devon nodded, and wiped his mouth with his napkin.

"And I shot the winning points in basketball," announced Ed, followed by spearing a piece of chicken from his plate and neatly placing it into his mouth.

Jana answered with a smile, "That's wonderful boys." Turning to Gloria, she asked, "Are you settling in all right, Gloria?"

Gloria swallowed a mushroom then replied, "Sure. My bedroom is beautiful. And the kids have been really helpful."

Devon and Ed smiled sweetly.

Whose children are these?

After using her napkin to mop up spilled milk in front of Ed's plate, Gloria asked, "And how was your day, Jana?"

After taking in a deep breath, Jana put down her silverware, and announced, "Devon, Ed…Gloria, I'm going to act in a movie that's being shot in our home."

Devon asked, "What's it about?"

Censoring her words, Jana replied, "A woman like me."

"Does she have kids?" Devon added.

"I'm afraid not."

Ed asked, "Does she play basketball?"

"Sorry. No."

Going back to their dinners, Devon and Ed seemed to lose interest.

Gloria, however, bounced off her chair like a trampoline artist. "How exciting! A movie being shot right here in this house?" She rested her hand over her heart. "After all these years, going back to acting. That's amazing!"

You can wheel me to my first scene.

Gloria gushed. "When do we start?" Putting her hand over her red lips, she said, "I mean, when do *you* start?"

Jana smiled. "In just a few weeks. So, while I learn my lines, I'll need you to look after the children."

"Is that difficult…learning lines?" Gloria asked.

"It was never a problem for me when I was a child." *However, I'm not a child anymore.* "And once shooting begins, you'll need to take full charge of Brian Jr. A movie set can be a dangerous place. There will be a great deal of equipment here, and I don't want him getting hurt."

"Of course. You can count on me, Jana." Gloria added with a gleam in her blue eyes, "I'll be right here."

****

That night, Jana sat under their ruby satin canopy bedcover, resting her head on the gold circular headboard. In contrast to her husband's checkered boxer shorts, she wore a silver satin nightgown. She stared ahead at the island fireplace then tapped a finger on Brian's muscular back.

He said, "I'm beat, babe."

She tapped again.

Turning around to face her, Brian asked, "What's wrong?"

"Simon came by today."

"That's nice."

Before Brian could turn back on his side, Jana said, "And he asked me to star in a movie."

"What?"

Reciting the lines she had written, edited, rewritten, memorized, and rehearsed, Jana said, "Honey, it's a good film and a terrific part. I'll be working with top notch people, and I won't have to leave home. Devon and Ed will be at camp. You'll be coming and going from meetings about the new mall chain in Dallas. Gloria and Theresa can take care of Brian Jr., and I'll be here in case anything goes wrong. Simon is staying in Rhinebeck with Cornelius, and he'll watch over me."

After a pause, Brian said, "I think you should do it."

This is the man who turns into a bear with no honey in sight whenever I mention my Hollywood days? "Come again?"

He put his muscular arm around her shoulder and kissed her cheek. "You've been in some kind of funk lately, Jan. Maybe the movie will help."

Shrugging him away, Jana said, "But you always told me the movies created all my problems, and being away from the business with you and the kids was best for me."

"Maybe I was wrong." He held her shoulders. "I know I haven't spent enough time with you lately. But my firm is finally kicking off, babe, and I want you to be happy. If this is what will do that for you, you have my blessing."

They shared a long, warm kiss.

Looking like a puppy brought in from the rain, Brian asked, "Are we okay?"

Shocked, suspicious, and relieved, all at the same time, Jana rested her head on her husband's strong chest. "I love you, Brian."

Brian's light snoring filled the room.

****

Over the next two weeks, Jana kept herself busy working out, learning lines, thinking about her character in the film, and taking care of Brian and the children. She also attended meetings at the Vanderbilt historic estate to plan her upcoming fundraiser for AIDS research and treatment.

The following Monday at nine in the morning, Jana

sat in front of a camera. Production had not yet begun on her movie. Jana was seated on a lumpy black leather seat in the local cable television studio. Clad in a burgundy business suit with shoulder pads, tear drop earrings, and a gold link bracelet, her hair was pulled back in a tight bun.

Sitting to the right of Jana was Chad Channing, the host of *Chatting with Chad*. The middle-aged, self-proclaimed local media star and three-time losing candidate for mayor wore a light blue leisure suit and matching shoes with a long gold chain hanging from his neck. His black toupee slid down his forehead, revealing a mound of bushy gray hair on the sides.

Reverend Rodney Charlton sat to Jana's left, wearing his minister's white color and black shirt, slacks, and jacket—in addition to a sanctimonious look on his forty-plus, well-fed face. He sat with one hand in his pocket, jingling his keys.

The theme song of *Chariots of Fire* by Vangelis played then Chad unleashed his capped smile at the camera. "Welcome once again to *Chatting with Chad*. I'm Chad Channing, your host." Shifting his gaze to camera two, Chad continued with his contact lens covered eyes glowing in the studio lighting. "Our guests today are onetime child star, Vassar College graduate, and Hyde Park resident Jana Lane. Joining Jana is Reverend Rodney Charlton, pastor of the Only Way to Heaven Church in Beacon, and host of the *Right Reverend Rodney Show* on this cable network." Turning to face camera three, Chad said, "Our guests are here to talk about the upcoming fundraiser for research and treatment of the newly labeled disease, AIDS, which as I understand it, is Acquired Immune

Deficiency Syndrome. Is that right, Jana?"

"That's correct," Jana answered.

Still looking at the camera, Chad said, "Jana, tell us about your efforts to assist those stricken with this disease, and why you seem to be fighting a lonely battle."

Jana replied, "Certainly. The kind staff at the Vanderbilt historic mansion have agreed to let us host our black tie dinner and fundraiser at their site one month from today at seven o'clock. The food, drink, and flowers are being donated by local merchants; local musicians led by Cornelius Chamberlain are playing free of charge; and the entire staff is made up of volunteers. So, one hundred percent of the money raised is going to AIDS research to find a cure, and to help those stricken in our area."

Chad nodded his head gravely. "Jana, I have heard the complaint that the president, governor, and even the mayor of New York City have done very little to help this cause. Many charitable organizations and churches have turned their backs. Why do you suppose that is?"

"I'll tell you why." Rev. Charlton waved his plump finger. "This disease, as I understand it, strikes only homosexuals." He offered a compassionate gaze to the camera. "And while we love our homosexual brothers and sisters, decent people must stand up against their sin."

Chad asked, "So, pastor, as a man of God, you believe the disease they call AIDS is the wrath of God?"

After a pompous nod, jiggling his pudgy cheeks, Rev. Charlton replied, "It is no different from God's punishment in the Bible."

Jana felt her face flame. "Rev. Charlton, medical researchers believe this disease has stricken heterosexuals in Africa. And I don't believe any illness is God's wrath against those who suffer from it. My son had the flu recently. I don't believe that was God's punishment against my child."

Rev. Charlton replied, "It may have been...given your penchant for supporting the homosexual lifestyle." He winked at the camera. "Or should I say, *deathstyle*."

"Rev. Charlton, one's inborn sexual orientation is not a *lifestyle*. And just as God loves all of us, and instructs us not to judge one another, we must love all humankind, and judge no one."

"Comment, pastor?" Chad asked, sitting on the edge of his seat.

Charlton's flabby face tightened. "God is very clear in the Bible about the sin of homosexuality. Stoning to death is the punishment. The same holds true for a woman marrying when she is not a virgin, and for committing the sin of adultery."

Meeting him eye for eye, Jana replied, "How many times have you been married, pastor?"

He squirmed in his seat. "Three."

"Read what the Bible has to say about divorce." She added acrimoniously, "You might also check out the section on how to sell your daughter to slavery."

Moving forward in his chair and nearly splitting his pants, Rev. Charlton said, "Mrs. Otley, Sodom and Gomorrah show that homosexuality is a sin, and brings down all those who associate with sinners."

"That story is about greed and rape." *You should know about greed, given your luxury home and car, no doubt paid for by tax-exempt donations to your church.*

Jana folded her hands over her chest. "Jesus ate with those cast off from society. He preached for us to love and care for our neighbors as ourselves. People with AIDS are our neighbors. Everyone has turned a back on them. Those suffering from this horrible, fatal disease so desperately need our help."

"In my church, we stand firm against sins abominable to God. You are not a member of my church, are you, Mrs. Otley?"

"No. *My* minister encourages us to follow Christianity by helping those less fortunate than ourselves."

"And on that note, we will take a commercial break." Chad continued with a frozen smile, "When we return, you'll meet a mother of four dancers...dancing pets that is. Stay tuned."

The moment the red light on the camera dimmed, Rev. Charlton dropped his plastered on smile, and leapt out of his seat. "Chad, I request a follow-up interview. I fear I came off a tad hostile."

Jana rose. "A minister advising others not to help the sick is more than hostile. In your words, it's an abomination."

"But I didn't say that!" Charlton replied like a child throwing a tantrum.

Chad ushered them to the studio door. "Thank you both for the visit. You were terrific. Let's do it again at the AIDS benefit, or perhaps at your place, Jana...a promo piece for your new flick."

Jana's eyes grew bulbous. "How do you know about the film?"

"Word travels fast." Chad opened the door, and an elderly woman with a cat, dog, parakeet, and goldfish entered the studio.

As they walked through the studio lobby, Rev. Charlton asked snidely, "Mrs. Otley, is your movie about the *victims* of AIDS?"

Stopping in her tracks, Jana said, "Hollywood is just as afraid of people with AIDS as you are, reverend. The film is a thriller."

"Chock full of sex and violence, I assume?"

"You assume wrong."

He scratched his bald head. "Fine. Then I may come by one day while you are shooting."

"It's a closed set."

"But surely it is not closed to a local *minister*, Mrs. Otley." The pastor executed a stiff bow then went on his way.

Jana went shopping, drove home, and put away her groceries while her blood pressure slowly dropped down to normal.

The president may pretend AIDS doesn't exist, and Reverend Charlton might demonize people with AIDS to raise funds for his church, but I won't forget about the victims of this horrible plague. I thought religious people were supposed to feed the hungry, heal the sick, house the homeless, and clothe the naked.

As the word "naked" reverberated in her head, Jana looked out the glass wall of her kitchen and saw Gloria—in a lemon bikini—splashing with the children in the heart-shaped pool. Brian stood at the edge of the pool in his work suit as Laura Branigan's "Gloria" played from the radio next to the pool. Jana ran through the French doors, like a firefighter heading for a burning building, and reached the pool quickly.

"Hi, Mommy!" shouted Devon and Ed.

Brian added, "Hi, babe."

Adjusting the strap of her bikini, Gloria said, "Hi, Jana."

"Hi, everyone." Feeling like a parent crashing a slumber party, Jana turned off the radio. "Brian, what are you doing home?"

He replied, "I came home to pack for Dallas."

"Gloria, can you help me with something in the kitchen?" Jana asked.

"Sure. Be good, guys." With Brian watching, Gloria leapt out of the pool as water droplets careened down her shapely legs onto the concrete floor. She grabbed a terrycloth robe from the cabana then followed Jana into the house.

Jana and Gloria walked through the kitchen French doors. "Gloria, I'm not a prude, but I wish you would wear a less revealing bathing suit around the children." *And around my husband.*

Gloria blushed. "Sorry, Jana. This is the only one I had."

"Please feel free to borrow one from my lower right dresser drawer—a one piece."

"I will. Thanks, Jana."

After Gloria went upstairs, Brian entered the kitchen. "How did your interview go at the cable TV station?"

"It went," Jana said, watching the children from the doorway.

"Are you angry with me?"

"No, of course not. I just sent Gloria upstairs to change. We have two small boys."

Brian burst out laughing. "You're jealous because I looked at Gloria in her bathing suit."

Jana stopped mid-seethe. "I am not."

"Yes, you are. My wife is jealous." Brian leaned in for a long, sensuous kiss.

"Brian, stop."

"Uh-uh." Brian picked Jana up in his arms, carried her out of the kitchen, and up the spiral staircase to their bedroom.

"Brian!"

Theresa, polishing the silverware in front of the kitchen television set, called after them, "Shh. Roxanna and Pedro are finally going to make love on my show."

They passed a surprised-looking Gloria, wearing Jana's one-piece bathing suit, on the stairs. Then nearly knocking over a Tiffany lamp in their bedroom, Brian gently placed Jana on the bed, lay on top of her, and showered her with kisses.

Jana wrapped her arms around his muscular back, and they enjoyed love in the afternoon.

An hour later, Jana and Brian kissed under the skylights in the front hallway.

"I'll miss you so much," Brian said with a tweak of her nose.

"As much as you'll miss, Gloria?" Jana asked with a smirk.

"Well, maybe not that much."

Jana slapped Brian's firm, round bottom.

He pressed her closer to his strapping chest. "Jan, you are the *only* woman for me."

They shared another kiss and hug.

Jana fought back tears. "Call me every day."

"Of course."

"And don't worry about me."

"Not possible."

Jana smiled. "I'll make sure the movie crew doesn't damage anything in the house."

Brian kissed her forehead. "Make sure they don't damage *you*."

She smiled. "Nobody can hurt me. I'm Jana Lane, remember?"

"Jana Lane *Otley*."

They shared a long kiss. Then Jana watched the limousine driver load the luggage into the trunk. Brian blew Jana a kiss, and mouthed the words, 'I'm yours, forever.'

After the car drove off, Jana went back inside the house. She missed Brian already.

****

The following week was a whirlwind of getting Devon and Ed off to summer camp, talking to Brian on the phone, attending AIDS fundraising meetings at the Vanderbilt estate, and attending pre-production meetings/wardrobe fittings/pre-publicity junkets in New York City for the film.

****

Two days later, Jana stood in her entrance hallway welcoming two men into her home. Wearing a lime blouse and teal Capri pants, Jana stood at the doorway with her mouth agape.

This is the most gorgeous man I have ever seen in my life.

Jason Apollo, thirty-four, with sculpted features and a perfect muscular body, smiled sweetly. Though one of the biggest box office movie stars, he had a sensitive, boyish quality that turned Jana, and everyone else, into putty. Jana stared at his sparkling blue eyes and thick blond hair. "It's nice to meet you, Jana. I'm a

fan. I'm Jason Apollo. I play the detective in the film."
His huge pectoral muscles peeked out of his open
flannel shirt. Tight jeans and hint of a southern accent
completed the perfect picture.

Jana's knees dipped. "It's very nice to meet you,
too, Jason. I'm Jana Lane." *Did I purposely forget
Otley?*

Jack Capello, fifty, craggy-faced, and thin with
yellow teeth and black fingertips, brought her back to
reality. "Can we come in?"

"Of course." Still unable to take her eyes off Jason
Apollo, Jana ushered them into the hunter green and
pale peach sitting room. She had seen Jason's picture
on television and in the newspaper, but having not seen
any of his movies, Jana was taken aback by his almost
supernatural beauty and boyish charisma. She was also
surprised at his height, not much taller than hers.

Nearly tripping over a ceramic vase from India,
Jana motioned for the two men to sit on the overstuffed
loveseat across from the fireplace. She sat opposite
them on a wingback chair, which sported pictures of
peaches and plums.

After refusing Jana's offer of tea, Jack rubbed the
bags under his red eyes then scratched his salt-and-
pepper crew cut. "As you know from our meeting in
New York, Jana, we have a tight deadline to shoot this
picture. So I've been working out as many details as
possible at pre-production. Your agent sent me pictures
of the property, but I need to see everything in flesh and
bones. My cinematographer, director of photography,
and assistant director are meeting me here in an hour to
check out locations. In the meantime, I'd like to look
around the house and the grounds."

So much for cozy small talk. "That's fine. My husband is away on business. The baby is in his bedroom upstairs with his nanny. And my housekeeper is in the kitchen." *While you look around, I'll keep staring at Jason Apollo.*

Jack scratched at the crows' feet on his face. "We'll need full access, but we'll try to keep the house and grounds as neat as possible."

"I appreciate that," replied Jana with glances over to Jason.

Jason looked at Jana as if she was the only person in the world. "You have a beautiful home, Jana."

Not as beautiful as you. "Thank you, Jason. I'm sure it's quite modest compared to your home in Los Angeles."

He smiled, revealing a row of perfectly white, straight teeth. "You might be surprised. My house in Malibu is pretty modest compared to some I've seen."

Dressed in a black turtleneck and jeans, Jack glanced at his battered watch. "Do you know your lines, Jana?"

She nodded. "My son's nanny has been a stern taskmaster."

"Good. I don't want to waste time rehearsing. We start shooting in two days. You two get to know each other." Jack rose from the loveseat and was gone.

Jana and Jason burst out laughing.

Jana asked, "Is he always so warm and fuzzy?"

"After our lunch meeting in LA, the waiter quit his job." Jason giggled. "But Jack's a good director. His pictures are top notch." He smiled at the possibility. "So, I guess we'll have to look to one another for pleasantries."

33

How pleasant. Realizing she was biting her lip, Jana recovered by asking, "Would you like some lunch?"

"We ate in New York City. What I'd love is a tour of your grounds."

"Sure. It's a beautiful day." *And it just got even more beautiful.*

Jana and Jason walked out the front door and looked through the two tall white columns at her five acres of land bordering breathtaking mountain views on one side, and twinkling blue Hudson River antics on the other. They walked around the house, passing the pool, cabana, hot tub, and tool shed then stopped at a garden near a small wooden bridge over a lake.

Taking in the rainbow effect of the magnolia, pansy, bloodroot, redbud, lilac, iris, hyacinth, daffodil, tulip, hydrangea, and pink azalea surrounding them, Jana said, "Isn't that an amazing smell?"

"You smell better," Jason said with a warm grin. Moving his strong nose near the hair at her shoulders, he asked, "Vanilla?"

Jana blushed like a teenager on her first date. "It's my shampoo."

"I like it." Surveying the grounds, Jason added, "This is beautiful, just like its owner. It's even nicer than Malibu."

Jana glanced at her wedding ring. "'The other man's grass,' as they say."

Looking down at the emerald-green, perfectly manicured lawn, Jason said, "I even like your grass."

After sharing a laugh, they walked over the small wooden bridge past a savory herb garden and aging oak trees. When they got to the riding stables, they rested at a wooden post fence. Jana waved to the groomsman feeding her three horses.

"Do you ride?" Jason asked with a twinkle in his eyes.

"Not as much as I used to," Jana replied.

Resting a boot on the fence post hosting Ed's birdhouse, Jason said, "You rode a horse to save your little friend Timmy in *The Cowgirl and the Bandit*...and in *Sugar and Spice*."

Jana raised an eyebrow. "You remember my old movies?"

He grinned like a kid with a frog hidden in his lunch box. "I have to admit, I had a huge crush on you growing up. I saw all of your movies."

"Now that you've met me, sorry to disappoint you."

"Who said I'm disappointed?"

Time to bring the hormones back in check, girl. "It's my turn for confessions. I've never seen any of your movies."

"You haven't missed much. I'm hoping this film convinces the public I can act."

She crinkled her button nose. "You're tired of being America's heartthrob?"

He replied with an earnest look on his handsome face. "I never wanted that."

Jana shrugged her shoulders. "Want it or not. You certainly got it."

They continued walking past a sweet-smelling peach tree leading to a forest of trees.

"Do you run through the forest like you did in *Jungle Girl*?"

Only in my nightmares. "Hardly ever."

Jason gazed at the thatched guest cottage in the distance with the mountains behind it. He took in a deep breath. "This reminds me of home."

"Where's home?"

"Kentucky."

"Did you live in the mountains?"

"Sure did. Just like in your *Little Girl on the Ranch* movie."

"What does your dad do?"

"He's a coal miner. And my mom is a housewife. I'm their only kid."

"They must be very proud of you."

He rubbed his square jaw. "Hollywood isn't their thing, I'm afraid."

"Coming from a theatrical family, I envy that."

"Like you said, 'the other man's grass.'"

"Do you see your parents much?"

A pained look filled his handsome face. "Things aren't the same when I go home. I've changed too much for them."

"Everybody changes."

"Not where I come from."

With the sun over them like a warm golden blanket, Jana and Jason continued walking.

"How did a kid from Kentucky become a movie star?"

The sun danced in his sky-blue eyes. "Myrna Buller."

"Your manager?"

"Myrna's more than my manager."

"I see." Jana felt like a gossip columnist. "Will she be visiting the set during shooting?"

"Yes. But it's not what you're thinking."

"How do you know what I'm thinking?"

He replied, "I have an affinity for understanding women."

"And for modesty."

They shared a laugh.

Jason said, "Myrna discovered me."

Smart woman. "How did she find you?"

"Myrna's career as a gymnast and marriage to a movie producer had ended. Looking for comfort from her family, she visited a cousin in Kentucky who dragged Myrna to a high school play, *Romeo and Juliet*, starring the cousin's daughter as Juliet."

"And you played Romeo?"

Jason touched the tip of his nose like a charades player. "I was absolutely awful in the play, but Myrna miraculously saw I had talent. By the time I graduated high school, Myrna had become a manager for actors. She remembered me and flew me to LA, let me live in her guest room, and paid for my acting teacher, speech coach, personal trainer, hair stylist, and even a surgeon to, as Myrna said, correct a few of God's little errors."

He did an amazing job. "And Myrna put together the package deal for our movie."

"Right. Everyone in the film is her client...except you. As you can imagine, she has a huge stake in the film's success."

"Especially since *you* are one of the stars."

Looking like a little boy whose mother took away his candy, Jason said, "Jana, it's not what you're thinking. Myrna and I are friends and business associates. Nothing more."

Not so smart a woman.

They stopped in front of the guest cottage.

Jana said, "I notice you don't travel with an entourage."

"That stuff's not for me."

"Is there someone special in your life?"

"Yeah, you."

Jana's heart skipped a beat.

His dimples gave him away. "As the detective in the film, I'm hot as hell for your character."

Ah, yes, the movie.

Motioning to the guest cottage, Jason asked like Tom Sawyer about to start a new adventure, "Can we go inside?"

"Sure."

Jana opened the door and led Jason inside. He surveyed the brown suede sofa bed, kitchenette with adjoining counter and stools, round wooden table and chairs, small windows with blue shutters, two red suede easy chairs on a woolen rug flanking a brick fireplace, and the adjoining closet and powder room.

"Does anyone live here?" asked Jason.

"Not presently."

"Can I stay here during shooting?"

Jana's eyes jettisoned out of her head. "You're joking."

"Actually, I'm totally serious. Caeneus Films has me booked into a fancy hotel in Chester, but this place is more my style. Plus, I'll be closer to the set." He winked at her. "And I'll be near you."

Jana replied, "Are you sure you don't want to stay somewhere more…opulent?"

"Absolutely." He sat on a chair by the fireplace. "Home sweet home." Jason added like a teenager requesting a late curfew, "Please, Jana?"

After processing the turn of events, Jana said, "Sure, Jason, you can stay here. Since Jack isn't planning any rehearsals, we can meet up and rehearse. I'm dying to talk to someone about my character's actions, objectives, and the emotional beats in our scenes."

He stood next to her, and pinched her cheek affectionately. "I have the feeling we will be talking about our emotions a great deal."

I wonder if a woman can buy a chastity belt in 1982.

Chapter 3

Over the next two days, Jana felt as if caught in a whirlwind during a hurricane. Amidst phone conversations with Brian and the two boys and taking care of Brian Jr., she attended AIDS fundraising meetings at the Vanderbilt mansion. She was also poked and prodded at final costume fittings. Finally, she helped Jason settle into the guest cottage while they rehearsed their scenes and discussed their characters.

The first day of shooting arrived. While Jack's promise to shelter the house may have been sincere at the time, it never happened. Cables, cameras, boom microphones, sound boards, monitors, dollies, sandbags, blankets, racks of costumes and accessories, carts of food and drink, and workmen wearing heavy boots took over the house. The great room was converted into mission central with a desk for Jack. Many minions—the director of photography, assistant director, cinematographer, lighting designer, sound engineer, costume designer, scenic designer, screenwriter, script consultant, casting director for extras, various producers, prop people, electricians, accountants, caterers, drivers, security to keep out the press, and executives from Caeneus Films—entered and exited constantly. The cerise-colored sitting room upstairs was converted into a makeup room with the three blue with rose inlay wingback chairs set up for the actors. Hylas, the makeup and hair artist, used the bookcases to store his grooming products, and the teakwood desk to line up his hand mirrors, water bottles, and blow dryers. The small crimson loveseat in the shape of a heart housed Hylas' Styrofoam coffee cup, candy bars, and chewing gum.

Jana sat on one of the wingback chairs wearing her costume—a satin nightgown and robe.

As he took the large rollers out of her hair, Hylas combed and teased her strawberry-blonde locks into a Christie Brinkley look. With his dark skin, bald head, and gold tunic and slacks, the thirty-year-old looked like a genie. "You won't need extensions...or even conditioning. Your hair is gorgeous with a capital g, honey."

Jana giggled. "Where have you been all my life, Hylas?"

"Doing hair and makeup in Hollywood for actresses nearly as bald as me," Hylas responded with his eyes raised to the gold chandelier.

"I'm glad you came east for this film," Jana said with a warm smile.

Applying her base makeup, Hylas said, "You have *some* cheekbones, honey. And those eyes are bluer than true."

"I like you, Hylas."

He picked up a blush brush. "Didn't you say that to your little friend Timmy in your candy striper movie before you saved him from the mad hospital administrator with the stolen surgical knives?" He took a sip of his coffee. "Does this mean we'll be, 'true blue friends forever'?"

Tom Strong, playing Jana's husband in the film, sat

down in the next chair. He wore his costume—burgundy pajamas and smoking jacket. With his brooding eyes and dark hair, ruggedly handsome features, tall height, muscular physique, and polite mid-Western cadence, Jana could see why the forty-year-old actor was so popular with middle-aged women. He winked at Jana. "Hylas, go easy on our leading lady. She was once America's sweetheart."

"She's still a sweetheart," Hylas said, popping the rest of a candy bar into his mouth.

Tom stretched out a hand to Jana. "Hi, I'm Tom Strong."

Shaking his hand, Jana replied, "It's so nice to finally meet you, Tom." *Before we do our scene in bed together.* "How was your trip from LA?"

"Fine," he replied, ducking out of Hylas' way. "My wife was supposed to come with me, but she had a last minute emergency."

"I hope everything's all right," Jana said.

Hylas smirked. "Look at that hunk of man. His wife will be just fine."

"And so will I," Tom said with a gracious smile. "The hotel is very comfortable."

Hylas pulled Jana's chin up with his thumb to apply lipstick. When he finished, he said, "Beautiful!"

"Thank you," replied Jana.

Tom explained, "He means his work."

"You know it, honey," said Hylas with a snap of his chewing gum.

As Hylas moved on to do her eye makeup, Jana asked her co-star, "How did shooting go earlier this morning?"

Tom replied, "Fine. We used the courthouse in

Poughkeepsie as my governor's office in Albany."

"Since you're already made up, would you like to rehearse our scene?" Jana asked.

Hylas waved an eyeliner. "Only if I can critique your acting."

"Deal," Jana and Tom said in unison.

"You two already sound like a married couple," Hylas said as he blew a bubble. "Let's take it from the top of the scene."

Jana and Tom ran their lines and discussed their characters' motivations with Hylas interjecting his impressions as he finished Jana's makeup.

Jana said, "Tom, let's create a back story for our characters. How and where do you think we met? When did we get married? Why do you think we haven't had children yet?"

Jana and Tom discussed their characters and the subtext of their upcoming scene as husband and wife as Hylas touched up Tom's makeup. Jana thought Tom's makeup was on a little too thick, but she assumed it kept the older actor looking appealing to his female fan base.

When Hylas was finished, he removed the gum and tossed a piece of candy into his mouth. "This actor talk is way over my bald head. I now pronounce you both hair dressed and made up. Now go in peace and prosper. I'll be on set for touch-ups."

After thanking Hylas, Jana led Tom to her bedroom, which seemed full of more equipment, people, and commotion than Grand Central Station. After Tom went inside, Simon Huckby stopped her at the doorway. Jana Lane's agent, wearing an olive-colored jumpsuit and plum scarf, kissed the air around his client. "Kiss, kiss, baby doll. I won't mess your makeup. Hylas is the best in the business."

Jana took his small hands. "Thank you for coming, Simon."

"Where else would I be on your first day of shooting?" He squeezed her hands. "Is everything all right?"

"So far so good," Jana replied taking in a deep breath.

"You still have it, baby girl. Nobody could ever out act you, and nobody ever will. Go in there, and show them how it's done by the best."

Jana put her arm around him. "I love you, Simon."

Simon clutched a hand to his heart. "Is that *your* nightgown and robe?"

"Yes, it is." Jana looked down at her clothing.

Her agent rubbed his hands together like a homeless man at a trash fire. "That's extra money for you! I'm going down to tell the producers right now."

What's ten percent of canary satin bed wear?

"Knock 'em dead in the scene." Simon wiped a tear from his indented cheek. "You're back where you belong, baby doll. And it's about time."

Jana walked into the bedroom and nearly fainted onto the marble floor at the sight of Gloria Covetry lying in her bed. "Gloria, what are you doing here?"

Gloria crinkled her tiny nose. "Hi, Jana. Isn't this fun?"

"Why are you in my bed?"

"Ryan O'Halloran, the assistant director, said I look just like you...when you were younger. So he asked me to be your stand-in while the crew set up all the whoseewhatsees for the lights and sound."

Jana's face turned beet red. "Where's Brian Jr.?"

"Theresa has him in the kitchen watching her soap opera," Gloria replied with an angelic look on her face.

Entering the room with his makeup kit in hand, Hylas whispered in Jana's ear, "You don't need any more rouge, girl."

Looking like a bull heading for the red cape, Jana made her way to Ryan O'Halloran. With the assistant director's short stature, stomach protruding over his red pants, pointy nose, green eyes, and large dimples, he looked like a department store elf. He said to a camera operator, "Unlike Jack, when *I* direct a film, I'm open to ideas from everybody, especially the camera operators."

"Pardon me, Ryan," Jana said, trying to keep her emotions in check.

Ryan stared at her chest. "Wow, you look terrific in that outfit."

Feeling hotter than an erupting volcano, Jana said, "Why is my child's nanny working as my stand-in?"

Ryan scratched his stomach. "She fits the bill. Unlike Jack, *I* try to cover all the bases, and make sure every actor has a stand-in."

"Is there a problem?" Jack Capello asked in director mode.

Jana replied, "Yes, Jack, I prefer my stand-in *not* be my child's nanny."

Jack replied dryly, "Fine." He turned to Ryan. "Use one of the techs from now on."

"But none of them resemble Jana," Ryan said with a tight jaw.

Lifting the Jana Lane porcelain doll from Jana's bureau, Jack replied, "There's only one Jana Lane.

45

Hence the doll. Are we done here?"

Ryan nodded into his chest.

"Thank you, Jack." Jana put the doll inside her closet for safe keeping then said to Gloria, "I'm sorry, but I hired you to be my nanny, not my stand-in, Gloria."

"No problem," Gloria said, rising from the bed.

As Jana took her place in the bed, she said, "You can stay and watch if you like."

"I would, very much. Thanks, Jana!" Gloria watched eagerly from behind one of the cameras.

Tom got into bed next to Jana. "Can I do anything to help?"

She cooled off. "Thanks, Tom. Everything's fine now."

Jack asked Ryan to call for quiet on the set. The slate was announced and cracked. A camera, surrounded by lighting equipment and a boom microphone, faced the bed for the long shot. Jana and Tom played the scene, where her husband cautions her about trusting her new young assistant. Both actors hit every mark and performed with depth and emotion. Their relationship as husband and wife was believable and interesting to watch.

As Jack called, "Cut," Tom started to cough, and Hylas handed him a glass of water.

Jana asked, "Are you all right, Tom?"

"Just a tickle in my throat," he replied, clearing his throat then finishing the water.

After the camera was repositioned for Tom's close-up, the second take was even better than the first. Tom tore into the material with passion and authority.

For the third take, Jana's close-up, she performed

with nuance and charisma. It was impossible for anyone in the room not to look at her. When the scene ended, the crew applauded, and Jack shouted, "Cut! We got it. Ryan, let's move to the next scene."

As the crew members scurried around the room to change lighting, sound, and props, Simon embraced Jana, standing next to the bed. "You were as perfect as always, girly. You made me proud."

Jana returned the hug then stepped into her bathroom. After shutting the door and walking past the towels with the O monogram, Jana sat on the marble surface of her jet tub, looked at herself in the wall-to-wall mirror, and wept.

I'm Jana Lane again!

Since movies aren't shot in sequence, as Jana changed clothes, the bedroom was set up for a scene much later in the film.

Fifteen minutes later, Jana, in designer jeans and a cream-colored blouse, sat on the cherry wingback chair as Hylas touched up her makeup and hair.

"A kiss with Jason Apollo," said Hylas, salivating over his mascara wand. "Honey, you're the envy of every straight woman and gay man in America."

Jana replied, "I'm sure I'll enjoy working with Jason as much as I enjoyed acting with Tom."

"How about you take Jason Apollo, and I'll get Tom Strong on the rebound?"

Jana giggled.

Jason Apollo, looking like a male model in a form-fitting dark blue suit, took his place next to Jana with a pad and pen in his smooth hands. Realizing no makeup in the world could make Jason Apollo more gorgeous, Hylas packed up his portable makeup case and watched from a corner of the room.

At this point in the screenplay, the ex-child star's husband has been murdered by her personal assistant who is now after her. As she seeks assistance from the detective, the two characters test one another, surrender information to each other, trap one another then finally admit their mutual attraction with a passionate kiss. Jana and Jason had rehearsed the scene at the guest cottage and were ready to totally inhabit the scene.

As Jack called for action, Jason turned to Jana and winked. "We're going to ace this, partner." And he was right. Their acting was top-notch. Jason proved to be much more than a matinee idol, and it looked as though Jana had never stopped acting.

On the first take, they teased and taunted one another, clung on to each other, and even improvised some new dialogue when they both acquiesced. Jana and Jason were in perfect harmony, like two dancers executing spins and lifts. Their timing was impeccable. And the emotional level of the scene was incredibly palpable.

At the end of the scene, Jason moved in for the kiss. Jana took in his full lips, square jaw, strong cheekbones, and sensitive eyes. She ran her hands through the smooth blond hair that fell over his forehead. When he put his arms around her, she wrapped her arms around his thick back, holding on to his rippling muscles. As their lips connected, they shared a warm, sensual, kiss as if they had been mates in a prior life. When the director yelled cut, they did the scene again, and again, nailing each take.

When they finished, Jason grinned. "I told you we'd be a great team."

After the successful day of shooting, Jana took a long bath then put on her apricot silk nightgown. She held, cooed with, kissed, sang to, and read to Brian Jr. then put him to bed.

Since her bedroom looked like the aftermath of the apocalypse, she sought haven in her oldest son's bedroom. Curling under the covers of Devon's bed, she picked up his spaceship phone and called her sons at camp. After she was satisfied they weren't starving, sick, sleep deprived, or homesick, she phoned Brian.

Brian answered on the first ring. "Hey, beautiful."

"How did you know it was me?" Jana asked.

"I didn't. But in case it was a beautiful woman, I wanted to be prepared," Brian responded with a naughty boy tone in his voice.

"How are the meetings going?" Jana asked, resting her head back on an alien pillow.

"Boring, but productive. I'll be a rich man once these malls hit every state."

"You're a rich man now."

"Thanks to you. It's about time I pull my share of the weight."

"What's mine is yours, and what's yours is mine, hubby."

Brian asked with concern in his voice, "Speaking of that, how's the film going?"

Surprised at her renewed energy, Jana said, "Brian, it's amazing. I didn't realize how much I missed it."

"Will we have to move to Hollywood?"

"That's part of the fun. Everything is happening right here." She rubbed her bare feet against the warm sheets. "I forgot how much fun it all is."

"I'm happy for you, babe."

"I had to fire Gloria as my stand-in."

"You what?"

"The A.D. selected her."

"I can see why. She resembles you."

So you noticed. "Gloria seemed to understand when I explained it wasn't a good idea."

"I bet you acted the crap out of your scenes today."

Jana replied, "My co-stars gave me a lot to play with."

"Is it *my* turn to be jealous now?"

Jana laughed. "Tom and Jason are good looking and sexy, but I'm a happily married woman."

"How many takes did you have to kiss Jason Apollo?"

"It was a long day."

"Answer the question."

Jana giggled. "Three. But who's counting?"

"You, obviously."

"Jason is gorgeous, but my guy's the only guy for me."

Brian said, "Jan, I'm glad you're having fun. Just be careful."

"Always." *I wish you were here.* "When are you coming home?"

"As soon as I can. I have to save the world by putting a mall in every community."

I miss you. "I love you."

"You're my heart, babe." He yawned.

She caught it. "Good night, my love." Jana hung up, pulled the sheet over shoulders, and rested her head on the pillow.

****

The ex-child star raced through the woods feeling

her assailant's breath at her neck. She ran around a large maple tree then another and headed for the lake on her property. A strong hand reached out and pushed Jana Lane into the water. As she gasped for air in fear...

"Jana, are you all right?" Gloria asked with a look of concern on her young face.

Jana took in some deep cleansing breaths. "I had a nightmare."

Gloria tied the belt around her pink cotton bathrobe. "Sorry to bother you, but there's a guy roaming around outside. I saw him from my bedroom window."

Wiping the perspiration off her forehead, Jana said, "It's probably Jason out for a walk."

Gloria's eyes darted to the window. "He's smaller than Jason Apollo."

"Go to the baby's room...and don't leave him." Jumping out of bed, Jana put on her bathrobe, and raced down the stairs.

Upon reaching the downstairs, Jana hurried from window to window in search of the intruder. When she arrived at the kitchen doors leading to the back of her property, Jana screamed at the sight of a man's face.

"I'm Trevor Masquer," he shouted with his face pressed against the glass. "Let me in."

Jana yanked open the French door like a prize fighter heading to the ring. "What are you doing here at this time of night?"

The young man bore an uncanny resemblance to John Hinckley with his brown hair, round face, deep set eyes, large forehead, square chin, wide nose, and broad shoulders. Wearing a tight black T-shirt, pants, and leather jacket, he strutted into the kitchen, and sat on a swivel chair in the breakfast nook. After rummaging inside the fruit bowl, he peeled a banana, took a bite, and said with his mouth full, "I wanted to see the place at night."

Standing next to him like a teacher scolding a misbehaving student, Jana replied, "I want to see good manners."

"It's part of my acting technique…to get the lay of the land before I shoot." He looked her up and down like a new car. "And to use sense memory to feel why I'm so infatuated with you."

Jana took a deep breath, and her shoulders dropped a few inches. "Trevor, we can talk about our characters and acting techniques, and rehearse our scenes tomorrow. I've had a long day, and I'd like to get some rest."

Trevor finished the banana and handed her the skin. Rising, he said, "I'll look around and make some connections with your personal things."

Jana's blood boiled like a pot of covered soup. "You will not!"

"Is everything okay?" Gloria stood in the doorway, clutching at her robe.

"What are you doing down here?" Jana asked with an eye roll.

Gloria replied, "Brian Jr. is sleeping. I wanted to make sure you were all right."

"I'm fine."

Trevor looked at Gloria like a shark meeting a sardine. "Hi. I'm Trevor Masquer."

Gloria goggled, like a backstage groupie at a rock concert. "Don't you play Jana's stalker in the film?"

"I'm the stalker," he said moving closer to Gloria. "And you *are*?"

Jana threw the banana skin in the trash. "Gloria is my son's nanny."

Putting his arm around Gloria, Trevor asked with seduction in his dark eyes, "Care to give me a tour of the place?"

Jana walked to the French door and flung it open. "Nobody is getting a tour of anywhere tonight. Good night, Trevor."

He walked to the door slowly and motioned to the hot tub. "I'm going to take a dip while looking up at your bedroom, Jana."

"No, you're not. Now please go back to your hotel."

He smiled, revealing capped white teeth. Jana wasn't sure if the young man's next comment was a come-on or a threat. "We'll have to change your mind about me, Jana Lane. You and I are going to become very close during this shoot. So get ready to rock and roll." Then he turned to Gloria. "Care to join me in the hot tub, Gloria?"

Jana replied, "Leave now, Trevor. I mean it."

Trevor's face was inches away from Jana's. "I thought we'd be friends like in your old movies. I guess you'll have to save me first." He winked at her. "Or maybe I'll save *you* from yourself."

After slamming the door after him, Jana heard Gloria say, "He's weird, but kind of sexy."

Jana stomped upstairs with a groan, checked on Brian Jr., tossed off her bathrobe, fell into bed, and stared at the ceiling in anger until her body gave up the fight, and she drifted off to sleep—an hour before her alarm rang.

****

The next morning, after a quick shower and a check on Brian Jr., Jana changed into her first costume—an avocado business suit with a diamond rope necklace and matching earrings—then headed to the food table in the great room—command central. The French doors to the patio and both fireplaces were covered with white sheets. The furniture was evacuated to the four-car garage. Card tables, folding chairs, and endless equipment filled the large room. People raced in and out like starving mice hunting for cheese.

Jana made her way to the bar, which was set up with a breakfast buffet. After helping herself to tea and fruit, Jana sat on a stool next to Tom Strong. Clad in a dark suit, Tom looked tired as he poured himself coffee.

"It looks like you didn't sleep much better than I did," Jana said. Thinking about their upcoming domestic argument in the film, Jana asked with a gleam in her eyes, "Are you ready for round one with me?"

Tom laughed. "Totally. I just spoke with my wife on the phone, so I'm primed."

"Art imitates life," Jana replied with a smile.

Hylas pulled Jana's hair away from her food. "Don't forget to come see me in the makeup room before we start shooting, gorgeous."

"Be right up," Tom said with a wink to Jana.

"Don't I wish," replied Hylas with a snap of gum, followed by his exit upstairs.

Jana said to Tom, "I like him."

"Me, too."

"Didn't you recommend Hylas for the film?" Jana asked as she speared a strawberry.

54

Tom nodded. "He's the best makeup man in the business."

"And it seems he likes to give actors the *business*."

They shared a laugh.

Jana noticed a sad look in Tom's dark eyes. *I hope he clears things up soon with his wife back in California.*

Sitting between them, snatching a raspberry from Jana's plate, and popping it into his mouth, Trevor Masquer said, "Use it."

"Pardon me?" Jana moved her plate away from Trevor.

Trevor explained like a pre-school teacher demonstrating the primary colors. "You two are playing husband and wife in the film. You have a scene coming up where you argue...over me." He pointed to Tom. "I overheard you say you had a brouhaha with your wife on the phone." Nudging Jana's shoulder, he said, "And Gloria said your hubby is out of town on...business. Take the anger you both feel toward your spouses, and use it in your upcoming scene."

Tom rose, towering over Trevor. "I don't think Jana Lane needs a lesson in acting from you."

"And I don't think our personal lives are any of your concern, Trevor," added Jana.

"But they *are*." Trevor put his arm around Jana's shoulders. "I'm your personal assistant." He pinched her cheek. "You're the love of my life, and my whole world."

Tom grabbed Trevor by the neck and lifted him in the air. "Buddy, you've obviously decided to be an ass. That's your prerogative. But if you don't behave yourself around this lady, I'll throw you through that

French door. Do we understand each other?"

Trevor wiggled free. "Suit yourselves. I have to get into makeup."

After Trevor was gone, Jana said, "Thanks, Tom."

Tom said, "That was nothing. Hylas will *really* put him in his place. I'm going up to watch."

Jana and Tom shared a laugh, then Tom mounted the spiral stairs.

"Hello, beautiful." Jason Apollo took Tom's seat. Since he wasn't shooting until the afternoon, he wore a tight polo shirt and jeans.

Blue is definitely your color. Any color is definitely your color. "Did you sleep well?" Jana asked as she dug into a grapefruit.

Stretching out his muscular back, Jason replied, "Like a baby. The guest cottage is my new nirvana." He helped himself to scrambled eggs. "Speaking of babies, how's yours?"

Jana gloated. "Brian Jr. has been wonderful through all this. Sleeping, eating, making his way around the upstairs, and napping without a tear. I think he likes the noise and elevated excitement in the air. He calls it, 'fun-fun.'"

"He's his mother's son." Jason winked at her. "Ready for our scene later today?"

"As ready as I'll ever be." *After my scene with Trevor, I should have no problem breaking down hysterically in your arms.*

"There's my bubala!" Myrna Buller was forty, short with frizzy red hair, tiny rectangular tortoise shell glasses, a fake button nose, and more mustache hair than a man who hasn't shaved in a week. She also wore more makeup than a cadaver. Myrna kissed Jason on each cheek. "Is everything going okay, bubala?"

"Fine," Jason replied with red cheeks. Then he said like a teenager whose father drove him to the prom, "Jana Lane, this is Myrna Buller."

Wearing a sequined sweatshirt and skin-tight leopard pants with a gold necklace that dangled over her enormous leopard pocketbook, Myrna wrapped her arms around Jana and squeezed her like an orange. "Of course this is Jana Lane. Hello, bubala. I'm thrilled you are doing *my* picture."

This woman was once a professional gymnast? With the sting of rose perfume in her nose, Jana somehow got free from Myrna's rolls of fat and came up for air. "It is a pleasure to meet you, Ms. Buller."

Myrna crinkled her face like a sandwich bag. "Ms. Buller, feh! Call me, Myrna." Though not Jewish, Myrna used Jewish idioms to sound more like a Hollywood manager. She sat on the stool between them. "So, isn't my boychik the best?"

Jason scratched at his blond hair. "Jana's terrific in the film, Myrna."

"Of course she's terrific. I only put together the best packages." Myrna squeezed Jason's bicep. "And look at the package I put together." Her cackle turned into a snort. She opened her handbag, and wiped her tiny nose with a handkerchief. "This film is gonna make *both* of your careers, believe me." She patted Jana's knee. "After the release, come talk to me. I have big plans for you."

"Of course you'll need to talk to Jana's *agent* about that." Simon Huckby stood next to Myrna, wearing a magenta and tangelo jumpsuit with a chartreuse scarf and matching waist pouch.

Myrna blew air kisses at his cheeks. "Simon, bubala. Our children are playing well together."

"I never had any doubt." After kissing Jana's cheek, careful not to damage his makeup, Simon squeezed Jason's other bicep. "And you're right about Jason's package, Myrna." Glancing downward, Simon added, "All of them." Simon giggled then helped himself to a plate of oatmeal, eggs, fruit, and a buckwheat waffle. "I love movie sets."

Like children home with their parents on a Saturday night, Jana and Jason rose from their seats.

Jana said, "It was very nice to meet you, Myrna. Thank you for coming, Simon. Duty calls upstairs."

"Make sure Hylas puts some clown white under your eyes, and pink rouge on your cheeks," said Simon between bites of his breakfast.

Jason grabbed a blueberry muffin, and was right behind her. "See you both later."

Wrapping a bagel and cream cheese into a napkin and sticking it inside her purse, Myrna called out, "I'll check on things when you start shooting."

Once they reached the upstairs, Jason went into the makeup room, and Jana headed for Brian Jr.'s room to check on him. After she was satisfied Brian Jr. was safe in his crib, she headed for Gloria's bedroom to see why his nanny wasn't with him.

Jana came upon Trevor Masquer listening at Gloria's closed bedroom door. Trevor stepped back as the door opened and Ryan O'Halloran, the assistant director, came out, closed the door behind him, nodded to Jana and Ryan then headed downstairs.

Trevor followed Ryan in a fury.

Jana knocked on the door. "Gloria, are you all

right?"

Gloria's voice sounded muffled. "Yes."

"Why aren't you with Brian Jr.?"

"He's sleeping. I'll check on him in a minute."

Noticing the strain in Gloria's voice, Jana asked, "Are you sure everything is okay?"

"Yes, I'm fine."

"Why was Ryan O'Halloran in your room?"

"Oh, the window was stuck, and I asked him to help me open it."

Is she holding back tears? "Next time tell me if there's a problem."

"I didn't want to bother you with something so trivial."

Jana replied, "Nothing is trivial when it comes to my family and my home. Okay, Gloria?"

"Okay."

"I'll be down the hall if you need me." Hearing water running, Jana shrugged her shoulders, and headed for the makeup room.

While getting into makeup, Jana noticed Hylas had again gone heavy on Tom Strong's makeup. *No doubt Hylas' way of staring at the handsome actor.*

After checking on Brian Jr. again, Jana headed downstairs to the cherry wood-paneled study. Since the room was the shooting location for the day, lighting and sound equipment were attached to the higher shelves of bookcases flanking the cherry wood fireplace mantel. Cables, sandbags, lighting poles, sound equipment, and technicians filled the room. Myrna Buller made her way around the room, checking in on her clients—Jason, Tom, Trevor, and Jack—like a mother hen feeding her chicks.

Jack Capello asked Ryan O'Halloran to call first positions. Ryan raised his eyes to the wood lighting fixture, and obeyed the order. Jana sat at the desk as Trevor took his place standing next to her. Tom Strong was behind the camera waiting for his entrance, standing next to Jack. Watching near the doorway were Simon, Myrna, Jason, and Hylas—makeup kit at the ready for repairs between takes.

Just as they were about to start the scene, Jack noticed a glare on Jana's face. So he asked Tony, the head lighting technician, to make an adjustment.

Ryan gloated. "That's why I wanted my stand-in for Jana."

Jack looked like a lion facing a kitten. "Can it, Ryan. Go help Tony with the lights."

After Ryan begrudgingly gave Jack's order to the lighting technician, he joined everyone in making small talk as they waited for the go-ahead to start the scene.

Wanting to speak with the assistant director about Gloria, Jana found Ryan O'Halloran near the doorway talking with Jason, Myrna, and Simon.

"It was just a documentary, but it was my first directing gig. Unlike on this set, everybody on *my* set seemed happy. I listened to everyone's ideas. You can ask your father, Jason. We did interviews with the coal miners in Lynch, Kentucky. Your dad gave us a lot of good information." He smiled at Jason. "Like you, he's a great guy. Shy. It took me some time to get him to talk. But I did, because I'm a good director." Ryan put his arm around Myrna. "We should discuss me directing your next package film, Myrna."

Before Myrna could respond, Jana interrupted Ryan's pitch. "Ryan, may I speak with you for a moment?"

"Sure." Ryan squeezed Myrna's shoulder. "We'll talk more later."

Jana brought Ryan to the large picture window. "Ryan, I saw you coming out of Gloria's bedroom earlier. Please understand Gloria's bedroom and Brian Jr.'s bedroom are off limits to the cast and crew."

Ryan shrugged his flabby shoulders. "Sure." Then his green eyes lit up like traffic lights. "Hey, Jana, do you have a director yet for your next film?"

Jana patted his arm. "Let's finish this film first."

Jack shouted for Ryan to call places.

"My master summons." Ryan called places, the cast and crew went to their first positions, and the slate was cracked.

The first take went well as Trevor came on to Jana, and Tom stood up to him. Equally obnoxious and frightening, Trevor was quite believable in the role. Jana met him beat for beat as she shunned his advances, and tried to reclaim their boss/employee relationship. Tom was solid as usual as the epitome of masculinity and valor.

Before the scene was finished, Ryan shouted, "Cut!"

Jack stormed over to him. "Ryan, what the hell do you think you're doing?"

Ryan rubbed his long nose. "The scene wasn't working, so I yelled cut."

"That's *my* job, Ryan. *Your* job is to *assist me*."

Ryan replied, "Jack, the three-point lighting and color balance are off. And the kid isn't pulling his weight."

Trevor's dark eyes ignited like charcoal. "You

have a problem with my acting, Ryan?"

"Yeah, actually," replied Ryan, standing between Jack and Trevor.

"And what would that be?" Trevor asked, ready to explode.

Ryan answered with a wave of his thick hands, "The bugabuga, scary, weirdo thing. Ever hear of subtlety? I'd take it down a peg."

Trevor said behind gritted, capped teeth, "I didn't realize you were an acting coach, Ryan."

"I'm not. Just a good director," Ryan said with his chin lifted.

Jack replied, "And the problem with that, Ryan, is *you* are not the director of this film."

Trevor added, "And, Ryan, given your inappropriate behavior on this set, you never *will* be a director."

"I just directed a documentary in Kentucky." Ryan pointed to Jason. "Just ask *him*."

Trevor said, "Documentaries in the sticks are your speed, Ryan. Leave feature film directing to the pros like Jack."

Grasping onto Jack's arm, Ryan said, "Look, Jack, you're not seeing this clearly. And I know why. But you have to give the kid some direction. If you don't, *I* will."

Jack yanked his arm free. "What you *will* do, Ryan, is shut your fat mouth."

Ryan looked as if he'd been stabbed with a dagger. "You can't tell me what to do, Jack."

"How's this for not telling you what to do?" Jack said, "Ryan, there's only one director on this set, and it's *me*. You can either be the A.D. on this film, or get the hell off my set."

Sulking like a child with a removed pacifier, Ryan went back to his place behind a lighting pole.

After a deep breath, Jack rubbed his leathery forehead. "Let's take five." Then he motioned for Trevor to follow him.

Taking advantage of the break to check on Brian Jr. in his playpen, Jana kissed her youngest child. Heavily involved with his colored shapes, he replied, "Biz-yee." As she left his bedroom, Jana noticed Jack standing with his arm around Trevor at the end of the hallway.

Given Ryan's on set comments about Trevor's acting, Jack must be giving Trevor a pep talk. Jana looked again at the two men, and was surprised to see Trevor's head on Jack's shoulder. *I guess I know how Trevor got the role.*

Once they were all back in the study, Jack asked Ryan to call for quiet then screamed, "Slate for Take Two." Once the slate cracked, Jack shouted, "And action!"

The second and third takes were even better than the first. Ryan's outburst seemed to have heightened the emotion on the set, which bled into the scene. Everyone on set, except Ryan, knew the scene was a winner. Jason winked at Jana. Myrna's chins nodded in satisfaction. Simon blew her a kiss.

Again Jack called for a break. Hylas took advantage of it by fluffing Jana's hair and powdering her forehead. He said as he worked, "Ryan's little outburst was all for naught. You three nailed it, hon."

Overhearing, Ryan said to Hylas, "My *little outburst* was considered collaboration on my set in

Kentucky."

"I'll stick to sets with a good director, like this one," said Hylas, with a snap of his gum.

Ryan replied, "How about *this* idea, Hylas? Why don't you stick to makeup and hair like a good little queen, and leave directing to the *real* men."

Before Jana could respond, Tom Strong, still in protector mode from the scene, put a strong hand on Ryan's sagging back. "Shouldn't you calm down, pal?"

Shrugging off Tom's arm, Ryan said, "Shouldn't you call your wife, Tom? She sees you so rarely. She must be worried about you."

Jack shouted, "Let's set up for the next scene, everyone." He tapped Ryan on the back. "You should have called that, but you were too busy arguing with the makeup guy."

With cast members, crew people, and visitors milling around them, Ryan asked Jack, "When do you think we'll be done filming today?"

"Why?" Jack replied.

"I have an appointment," Ryan replied with a smirk.

"You never could keep it in your pants, could you, Ryan?"

"My appointment *is* with a beautiful young woman, but it's not like that."

"What's it *like*?"

"She's a local reporter."

Jack's eyes narrowed. "This set is closed to the press. We'll do press conferences when the film is in the can."

"But she wants to hear about the experience of filming from the perspective of an assistant director on his way to becoming a director." Ryan ran his thick fingers through his black hair. "And I have a lot of stories to tell her....as you can imagine."

After a pause, Jack said, "We should wrap by seven." Jack revealed his yellow teeth. "Hey, Ryan, be careful."

"Always, Jack."

Jack called out, "Let's hustle, people. Time is money!" Then he turned to Ryan. "You should have said that, Ryan."

Jana, Jason, Tom, and Trevor headed for the great room like school children asked to stay together on a class trip. At the costume rack, the wardrobe mistress handed Jana and Jason their costumes for the upcoming scene, and they headed for the bathrooms to change. Jana came out looking beautiful in a white silk blouse, red velvet skirt, and pink cardigan with pretty gold earrings. Jason was equally stunning in a pin-striped blue suit that perfectly framed his sculpted body.

Tom and Trevor changed into their street clothes and handed in their costumes. Then all four actors headed back to the study.

At the study doorway, an assistant to one of the producers stopped her. "Excuse me, Miss Lane. Your minister would like to talk to you."

Rev. Heather is here? "Where?"

"On the sun porch."

"Thank you." Jana walked into the four-season sun room, and found Rev. Rodney Charlton rocking on the large rose print white glider.

With a smile on his round face, he raised a pudgy hand like a king expecting his ring to be kissed. "Hello, Mrs. Otley."

Standing over him with a look of disbelief on her made-up face, Jana asked, "Rev. Charlton, what are you doing here?"

Folding his hands together as if in prayer, he responded, "I told you at the cable television station I would be dropping by."

"But why?"

"To check on your movie, of course. It is my role as spiritual leader of this community to ensure the film's content is…appropriate for our little village."

Sitting on one of the white wicker rocking chairs, Jana said, "Rev. Charlton, you are not my minister, and the village is run by civil law, not by your church's rules."

He pursed his lips. "Something to hide, Mrs. Otley?" He crinkled his wide nose. "I hope this isn't *that* kind of movie."

After counting to ten, Jana replied, "The film is a psychological thriller loosely based on the John Hinchey case."

He folded his fat arms across his flabby chest. "Sounds like smut to me." Rising and walking past her, the reverend said, "I'd like to watch some of the shooting."

"I told you at the cable television station, this is a closed set."

With a stern look on his round face, Rev. Charlton said, "This set's shooting approval was granted by the town board members, many of whom are my congregants." He ran his hand over his bald head. "I wouldn't want your shooting permits to be revoked due to something I might say in my Sunday sermon…perhaps about the dangers of Hollywood infiltrating our community."

A technician called Jana to the set.

She threw her arms in the air. "All right, follow me." Jana walked to the study with Reverend Charlton salivating at her heels like a pit bull.

Jana entered the room and checked her lines in her script.

After inspecting the study, Reverend Charlton stood with Simon and Myrna, questioning them about the film's language, sexual content, anticipated rating, and personal lives of the leading actors.

Gloria entered and watched from a corner of the room.

Is that a tear in her eye? Reverend Charlton seemed to notice, too.

Reverend Charlton signaled Gloria, and they stepped out of the study together.

Jason was seated on a gold wingback chair near the fireplace. Jana took her seat opposite him on an identical chair. Technicians darted around them like laser beams as Hylas touched up their make-up.

Jason hardly needs a touch-up.

As Jana sat waiting for Jack to call for action, she looked up at Jason's encouraging face. She again was taken aback by his incredible beauty.

Reverend Charlton and Gloria reentered the study.

Jack called for quiet and action. Jana and Jason played the scene, where the detective notifies her of her husband's death. Jason delivered his lines with warmth, vulnerability, and obvious affection for Jana. In turn, Jana listened then reacted with deep emotions, conveying shock, loss, fear, and hysteria while being comforted by the man she trusted. Jana clutched onto

Jason with such force, her fingernail accidentally tore a hole in his jacket.

"Cut!" Jack hollered.

While the wardrobe woman repaired Jason's jacket, Jana noticed Reverend Charlton step out of the study again, this time with Ryan O'Halloran.

After the two men returned, and the jacket was mended, Jack called for slate and action for take two. Jana and Jason did the scene two more times. Each take was more realistic and heart-wrenching than the next, and each appeared as if it were the first time Jana was given the sad news.

After the third take, Jack shouted, "Cut! It's a wrap. Ryan, let's move on to the next location."

Jana wiped the tears from her cheeks.

Jason placed his hand on the side of her face. "You're amazing."

"You're not so bad yourself, partner."

"You make me better," he said with adoration in his true-blue eyes.

They shared a smile as again people hurried around the room like ants after a picnic.

Suddenly, Jana heard a loud crash followed by a scream. Leaping from her chair, she followed the horrified gazes of the others in the room to Ryan O'Halloran lying motionless on the floor with a Fresnel tungsten shuttered light next to his head, and blood dripping from his scalp onto the hardwood floor.

Chapter 4

After putting a mirror under Ryan's nose, Jack ordered everyone out of the study and into the great room while Jana phoned for an ambulance.

Upon exiting the room, Myrna said to Jason, "Don't let them stop shooting the film, bubala!"

Simon said to Jana, "Finish this film no matter what happens, baby doll!"

When the ambulance arrived, Jack directed the EMT workers to the study. The emergency medical technicians pronounced Ryan O'Halloran dead and left the property.

Next, the coroner and the detective arrived at the same time and conferred in the study.

After checking on Brian Jr., Jana cornered Tony, the head lighting technician, in the hallway outside the study. Tony, a small, wiry man with long, curly black hair and a Roman nose, shuffled from foot to foot.

"Tony, do you know what happened?"

"I'm totally baffled, Miss Lane."

She offered him a strained smile. "Please, call me, Jana." Recalling Ryan's argument with Jack and Trevor, Jana asked, "Tony, who set up that light for the last take?"

"*I* did. I set *all* the lights. And that light, like all the others, was attached firmly to the unipod." Tony waved his hands in the air like an orchestra conductor. "It was a brand new light. I checked it myself. There's no way it could have fallen."

"But it did," Jana said.

Tony fought back tears. "And I feel *terrible*. Has anybody notified Ryan's next of kin?"

"Jack said Ryan was divorced, and his parents were deceased. Jack phoned Ryan's sister."

Tony put his head in his small hands. "How could this have happened?"

In addition to the actors, the study was full of crew members and visitors. "Tony, was there a time when you weren't near that light…when someone could have tampered with it?"

"You mean intentionally dislodge it?"

She nodded.

Tony shrugged his narrow shoulders. "When Jack asked us to reset between scenes, I was running around like a lunatic, changing and focusing the lights. I guess somebody could have tampered with the light without me seeing him." Looking like a child afraid of a spanking, Tony said, "I better call my wife. She'll be crazy worried if she hears about this."

"Of course, Tony. Use the phone in the great room." Jana walked back inside the study and looked again at the fallen light.

"Mrs. Otley." Lieutenant Mario Rivera reentered the room and stood at Jana's side. The detective had raven black, tight, curly hair, smooth olive skin, and a strong nose. Due to a severe case of dandruff, in his dark suit he appeared to have come from outside in the snow.

"Hello, lieutenant," Jana said.

Rivera scratched the back of his head, dislodging

more dandruff flakes onto his broad shoulders. "I was against issuing the permits for this film to shoot in Hyde Park. I feared something like this might happen. They didn't listen to me at the town hall."

Jana replied, "I'm sure the producers had no idea something like this would happen."

"So I heard." After rechecking the various pieces of lighting equipment, he said, "I spoke with them, your director, and the head of the lighting crew."

Jana asked, "Shouldn't you be taping off this room as a crime scene?"

"I don't think so."

"Why not?"

Rivera raised his dark eyes to his bushy eyebrows. "With so many people in and out of here, it's already been contaminated. Besides, after talking to the coroner and checking the scene, I'm pronouncing this an accidental death. Jack Capello said this type of accident happens all the time on film sets. That's why film companies carry high insurance." He exhaled deeply. "The lighting guy probably forgot to tighten a bolt or screw."

"That's not what he told me."

"He would cover his butt, wouldn't he, Mrs. Otley?" Rivera began to leave.

Jana blurted out, "Ryan O'Halloran had an argument with Jack Capello, Trevor Masquer, and Hylas Summer."

He looked at her skeptically. "And you think one of them killed O'Halloran?"

"I didn't say that."

"Then what are you saying, Mrs. Otley?"

"I think there is more to this than meets the eye."

Rivera said, "Mrs. Otley, as you know, I come from New York City. I can sense a murder crime scene when I see one. This isn't it."

She looked him square in the eyes. "That's what you told me two years ago, and you were *wrong*."

"I don't think I'm wrong this time."

"Because you still believe I'm a hysterical actress who can't tell fact from fiction?"

He ran a hand through his tight curls, and it snowed over his broad back. "Mrs. Otley, I don't want to see you suffer a…see you get upset again."

Jana's back stiffened. "So you won't be investigating this?"

Heading to the doorway, Rivera replied, "I'll talk to Mr. Masquer and Mr. Summer, and anyone else downstairs who may have seen or heard anything. I'll also get someone to fingerprint that light. If nothing checks out, I'm filing my report."

"I think you're making a mistake."

He turned to face her. "Mrs. Otley, this isn't *The Girl Detective*. This is real life."

After Rivera left, Jana sat on the window seat with her eyes shut tight and her fists pressed against her forehead.

"Are you all right?" Jana opened her eyes and looked over at Jason Apollo sitting next to her.

Jana rubbed her sore temples. "Is it total bedlam downstairs?"

He looked at her with concern on his handsome face. "You didn't answer my question."

"Lieutenant Rivera and I have a history."

Sitting back against a throw pillow, Jason said, "I talked to Rivera for a while. He seems pretty thorough.

He was interviewing Hylas when I came up here looking for you."

"Why did you come up?"

Jason rubbed his large shoulder against hers. "Because I like you."

Somehow they shared a laugh.

Jana asked, "Is Jack suspending filming for tomorrow?"

"I don't think so. Jack said he's going to dedicate the picture to Ryan." He ran a thick finger across her chin. "Will you be okay to shoot?"

She swallowed hard. "I hope so."

He looked like a puppy with a ball in his mouth. "You want to rehearse tonight?"

Feeling miles away, she said, "I'd like to replay in my mind exactly what went on in this room today."

Jason tapped his head. "Then you need my instant replay machine." Rising, he added, "Come to the guest cottage for dinner. We can compare memories."

She said solemnly, "Jason, I don't think this was an accident."

"How do you know?"

"Call it a sixth sense, women's intuition, or whatever you like."

His thick blond hair fell over one eye. "I'll call it, the return of Jana Lane." Jason kissed her forehead, and left the room.

Summoning up her strength, Jana rose from the window seat and walked to the hallway. After checking on Brian Jr., she heard voices coming from Gloria's bedroom. Jana noticed Gloria's door was open. Standing at the doorway, she saw Trevor Masquer sitting on the bed with his arm around Gloria. Jana cleared her throat.

Gloria jumped up. "Jana, hi. Trevor and I were just talking about what happened to Ryan O'Halloran." Seeing the stern expression on Jana's face, Gloria handed Trevor his leather jacket, and pushed him out the door. "Thank you for speaking with me, Trevor. I appreciate it."

Lingering at the doorway, Trevor said to Gloria, "Are you sure you're all right?"

Gloria forced a smile. "Yes, sure, goodbye, Trevor."

After taking another look at Gloria, Trevor walked by Jana, and left.

Jana entered the pumpkin-colored room and stood next to the pumpkin canopy bed. "What's happening with you and Trevor, Gloria?"

Flitting around the vanity like a moth, Gloria replied, "Nothing."

Jana meant business. "Gloria, Trevor was listening at your bedroom door this morning before Ryan came out of your room. I've noticed the looks between you and Trevor. What's going on?"

Wringing her hands into her pink chiffon blouse, Gloria said, "Ryan walked by my room. He heard me crying, and he offered to help."

Sitting on the bed, and patting the spot next to her, Jana asked, "Why were you crying?"

Gloria sat next to Jana on the bed, and burst into tears. "I'm such a fool."

Jana held the girl in her arms, as Gloria wept. "Gloria, did Trevor hurt you?"

"No, Trevor was sweet and comforting."

"I don't understand."

"It was horrible. His stale breath, ugly face, greasy hair, fat body."

A light bulb went off over Jana's head. "Ryan O'Halloran! Did he force himself on you?"

Gloria pulled away, and tears streamed down her cheeks. "I let him do it." After a pathetic laugh, she added, "How sick was that?"

Jana took a tissue from the night table and wiped Gloria's tears. "Why, Gloria?"

Gasping in air, Gloria said between sobs, "He...told me...he could...get me into...the movie...business."

Jana exhaled a long sigh. "Gloria, why didn't you tell me you wanted to be in show business?"

"I didn't know. But after seeing all this excitement, and watching what you do, I decided to be an actress...like you. Ryan told me he could make that happen if...I was 'nice to him'. He said he had plans to direct his own films one day, and he was someone I should get to know."

Jana's fists tightened. "Gloria, that's not the way to get into show business. It takes time to learn your craft and to meet reputable people who will help you, not *use* you."

"That's what Trevor told me."

"How does Trevor fit into all this?"

"He overheard Ryan and me this morning. He must think I'm a total slut." Gloria wailed. "I'm such a moron!"

Taking another tissue and wiping Gloria's tears, Jana asked, "Gloria, did Ryan use protection?"

Gloria nodded.

"Thank goodness." Jana lifted the girl's chin. "And

you're sure Ryan didn't force himself on you?"

"In some ways, it would have been easier if he had."

Jana nodded. "Gloria, what you did was stupid. You should never do that again. Do you understand?"

"I do *now*."

"What Ryan O'Halloran did was vicious and deceptive." After a shaky breath, she added, "But he obviously won't be confronted with it." Rising, Jana said, "However, we need to tell someone besides Trevor Masquer."

Gloria rose and clutched at Jana's shoulders. "Please don't tell my mother, or anyone, even Brian. Please, Jana!"

"Won't Trevor talk about it?"

"He swore not to." Gloria wept again. "Trevor's a really nice guy." She pounded her fists against her head. "He must think I'm a total loser. And he's right!"

Jana took the young woman by her shoulders. "Gloria, we all make mistakes. The secret is to learn from them, and never make the same mistake twice. From now on your *only* role in this house is as B.J.'s nanny."

Gloria nodded then slowly walked into her bathroom and shut the door.

After making sure Gloria was all right, Jana went downstairs to try to calm down the remaining cast and crew members. Jack verified they were indeed planning to continue shooting the next day since "time is money."

Once everyone was gone, Jana went into the kitchen and phoned Devon and Ed from the phone on her desk. Hearing all about their basketball and soccer tournaments, swimming, tennis, and boating somewhat relaxed her.

Next, she called Brian who wasn't there. *I really need to talk to you, Brian!* After leaving a message to call her back, Jana went upstairs and changed into her Vassar sweatshirt, jeans, and sneakers, and pulled her hair back in a ponytail. After checking on Brian Jr. and Gloria and heading downstairs, she walked across her patio, gardens, riding stables, and woods following the lake to the guest cottage.

Standing in front of the door of the cottage, and hearing Roberta Flack's "Making Love," Jana laughed in spite of herself.

Every straight woman in America would envy me, and here I am wearing a sweatshirt, jeans, and sneakers to have dinner with Jason Apollo.

Jason answered her knock on the door, and welcomed Jana inside the guest cottage. Once she was seated comfortably on the red suede easy chair next to the fireplace, and sipping a cup of vanilla blackberry herbal tea, Jason took the seat next to her and smiled.

"Did I do something funny?" Jana asked.

He replied, "This is really nice."

"What?"

His blue eyes reflected the lit fireplace. "Being here with you."

Jana couldn't help but notice the muscles bulging out of Jason's T-shirt and exercise pants. "Have you been exercising?"

He nodded and his blond hair fell over his forehead. "At a gym in town."

"The women must have gone crazy."

"Not a problem. You haven't lived until you work

out wearing a sunhat and sunglasses."

Jana laughed. She took a sip of tea. It felt warm, savory, and soothing.

"Feel better now?" he asked.

"Yes, but I'll feel even better after we've eaten. Did you take us something from the film shoot?"

"No way." Jason made his way to the kitchenette, where he peeked into the covered pot on the oven. "I went shopping and made everything myself. We're having fillet of sole almandine, three-cheese baked potatoes, and baby greens with roasted beets and raspberries."

Jana's jaw dropped to her herbal tea. "Where did you learn to cook like that?"

"My mother taught me when I was a kid back in Kentucky."

Jana joined Jason in the kitchenette area. "I hope I'm not prying, but I wonder, why is it you said things aren't comfortable when you visit back home? I understand you've changed, but there has to be more to it than that."

He shrugged his strong shoulders. "I felt like a stranger in a familiar place. I guess my folks didn't like the new me."

What's not to like? "I guess Kentucky *is* very far from Hollywood, California."

"You have no idea." Jason spiced then re-covered the pot. "Dinner will be ready soon."

"Jason, there's something I've been dying to ask you."

"Yes, I'll marry you."

She hit his shapely bicep playfully. "Tell that to my husband."

"I would, but he's never around."

"I just left a phone message for him."

"Good, tell him to call me next."

She smiled and leaned against the kitchenette counter. "I hope you don't think I'm nosey—"

"Too late." He tweaked her nose.

She giggled. "I've been wondering why you aren't married, or living with someone." Surprised her throat was dry, Jana took another sip of tea. "I've read in the newspapers about your relationships with various actresses, but none of them seem to pan out. Were they made up by Myrna or your P.R. person?"

Folding his strong arms across his wide chest, Jason said with a smirk, "You're asking if I'm gay?"

Trying not to sound defensive, Jana said, "Which would be great." *That came out wrong.* "I mean, that would be fine with me." *How about sticking your entire leg in your mouth?* "I mean, Simon is gay, and I love Simon."

"Simon's not my type."

She turned ruby red. "I'm making a mess of this, aren't I?"

"But it's so much fun to watch."

They shared a laugh.

Jana said, "Of course whatever you are…or aren't…is none of my business." *But knowing you are gay would sure help my out-of-control libido.* "I guess I have a curious nature."

He rested his warm hand on her shoulder. "Jana, I'm not gay. I'm not attached. And I understand you're a wife and mother. No boundaries will be crossed here." Jason winked. "Unless you cross them." Opening the oven, he said, "Now, dinner is served."

After eating a sumptuous dinner, and rehearsing their scene for the next day, Jana and Jason rested on the brown suede sofa with their feet up on the large leather storage trunk opposite.

Jana said, "You are a very good actor."

"Right back at you."

"I mean, you are so much more than the critics give you credit for."

"Hopefully, this movie will prove that."

She looked into his gorgeous face. "The way you listen and react in a scene is totally believable. You let off this current of energy when you act. It's hard to take my eyes off you."

"My scene partner brought out the best in me."

I sure felt our attraction…as the characters. Smiling, she added, "Jason, thank you for the amazing dinner and powerful rehearsal."

"Not to mention my stimulating company."

"That goes without saying."

"Obviously."

She kicked his shin lightly, and they giggled. *Time to start the investigation.* "But now—"

"Now, Jana, the girl sheriff, wants to talk about what happened on set today."

Jana stared into the fire. "Do you think Ryan's death was an accident?"

"I haven't really thought about it."

"I've been thinking about nothing else."

"And?"

She sat up straight. "I think it's too much of a coincidence that Ryan argued with Jack, Trevor, and Hylas today before he was hit with that light."

"Don't forget Tom."

Jana hit her forehead with the palm of her hand. "That's right! As I recall, first Ryan and Jack had words about Ryan trying to direct the scene."

"It's not unusual for an A.D. to have aspirations to become a director, especially since Ryan has already directed a documentary. He interviewed my dad who said Ryan was a good director."

Jana bit her lip. "But it's *not* usual for an A.D. to try to take over like that, especially with a strong-willed director like Jack."

"True."

She squeezed her eyes shut. "And didn't Jack mention something to Ryan about, 'not being able to keep it in his pants'?"

Jason nodded. "That was probably a dig about Jack's wife."

"What about Jack's wife?"

"According to Myrna, who knows everything about Hollywood by the way, Ryan had 'relations' with a number of married women in Hollywood, including Jack's wife. Obviously, it caused quite a riff between Jack and Ryan."

"Then why did Jack hire Ryan to assist him in the movie?"

"If you believe the gossip columns, which I never do, Jack and his wife have separated. So maybe Jack got over it."

Sitting up on her knees, Jana said, "Ryan's appetite wasn't only for married women. He was also interested in Brian Jr.'s nanny." *I'll keep my word, Gloria.* Jana added, "And Ryan said he had a date with a reporter who I assume was female."

After a few moments of thoughtful silence, Jana

and Jason said in unison, "Are you thinking what I'm thinking?"

Jana said it first. "Ryan's comment about the reporter was a cloaked threat to expose his affair with Jack's wife."

Jason tapped her shoulder. "Jana, before you call Lieutenant Rivera and ask him to arrest our director, Jack wasn't the only one who had it out with Ryan."

"That's right!" Jana slapped her hands together. "When Tom Strong told Ryan to lay off Hylas, Ryan mentioned something about Tom never seeing his wife. Do you think Ryan was sleeping with *Tom's* wife, *too*?"

Jason unleashed his dimples. "What did Ryan have that *I* don't have?"

Jana slapped Jason's knee playfully. "Tony, the lighting man, is positive that light was attached to the pole properly. Jack and Tom had easy access to it during our breaks and set-ups."

"So did everyone else."

"That's right. And people were coming and going from that room all day, including my nanny, that horrible Reverend Charlton, and even Ryan himself. Now I'm even more convinced somebody tampered with that light." She sat back on the sofa. "Rivera won't investigate this. We have to do something."

Taking her hand in his, Jason said, "And we will. Tomorrow on set, we'll look and listen to everything and everyone. Then tomorrow night, we'll compare notes."

Jana smiled. "Like *Nick and Nora*?"

He squeezed her hand. "Uh-uh. Like Jason and Jana."

After Jason walked Jana back to the house and said

goodnight, she found Trevor Masquer sitting on the loveseat in her hunter green and pale peach sitting room. Coming to stand in front of the fireplace, Jana asked, "Trevor, what are you doing here?"

Putting his hands inside the pockets of his leather jacket, Trevor said, "I *was* talking to Gloria, until she went upstairs to change Brian Jr." Trevor unleashed his usual smirk. "How was your date with Jason Apollo? Is he as hot as they say in the rag papers?"

"We were rehearsing."

"Whatever you say."

Sitting on a leaf-patterned wingback chair, Jana said, "Trevor, I'm quite a bit older than you."

He slumped back and spread his legs. "But I wouldn't kick you out of bed."

"And over the years, I've learned people with a cocky attitude don't get what they want."

Trevor slid to the edge of his seat. "Is that why you don't like me?"

Flustered, Jana replied, "I don't really *know* you."

He put a hand on her leg. "We can fix that pretty quickly."

Jana removed his hand. "Actually, I *would* like to get to know you better, Trevor."

"Now you're talking, baby." Trevor's dark eyes glistened. "What would you like to know about me?"

Why you are so obnoxious for one. "When did you realize you wanted to be an actor?"

He laughed. "When my parents applauded after I recited my first nursery rhyme."

Jana sat back in her chair. "And your parents supported your ambitions?"

"Not at first, but after they got used to the idea,

they were cool with it."

"And they paid for you to go to college?"

He nodded. "Then to an acting conservatory in LA, strictly method. After that, I was in a touring theatre repertory company for a year. We did classic and contemporary plays."

"What was your first film role?"

"This is it."

Remembering Trevor and Jack together in the hallway, Jana asked, "Did you get the part by way of the casting couch?"

Trevor glared at her. "Absolutely not."

Running a hand through her strawberry-blonde locks, Jana asked, "Why did you become so defensive when Ryan O'Halloran criticized your acting on set yesterday?"

Trevor's deep set eyes took on a dull stare. "Ryan O'Halloran was a pathetic excuse for a human being." His jaw tightened. "And I don't care if he's dead."

He's cracking. Keep up the pressure, Jana. "That's a pretty severe reaction to a critique on your acting. Isn't it, Trevor?"

Trevor leaned forward and rested his elbows on his knees. "It was personal between Ryan and me."

"Were you lovers?"

"No way!"

"Then what?"

"We had a history."

"In what way?"

He locked eyes with Jana. "Why should I tell you?"

"Why *shouldn't* you? You're in my home, playing a supporting role in my film, interested in the nanny I hired, and telling me we should get to know one another better."

He swallowed hard, and looked down at the mosaic of peaches and strawberries on the rug. "Ryan manipulated Gloria."

"Gloria told me. What does that have to do with you?"

"I like her."

"Since you met her two days ago, that's not really a *history*."

He dug his leather boot into the rug. "What Ryan did to Gloria, he's done that before."

"With who?"

Trevor looked up, and Jana noticed tears brimming in his eyes. "With my mother."

Jana tried to put the pieces of the puzzle together. "Your mother had aspirations to be in show business?"

Trevor clenched his fists. "My father could have helped her, but he wanted her to stay home and be a housewife. Ryan offered her a ticket out. And she bought his line about becoming a big director one day. It destroyed her marriage to my father."

"Is your father in the movie business?"

He nodded. "But he didn't get me this part."

Jana softened her approach. "What happened to your mother, Trevor?"

"The usual pattern. Just like Gloria. Ryan O'Halloran has a long list of women whose lives he's ruined." He rose in a rage. "I'm glad Ryan was stopped. He was toxic."

Jana stood and met his gaze. "Were you the one who stopped him?"

Trevor recoiled as if punched in the stomach.

Joe Cosentino

"What do you mean?"

"Did you tamper with the light that killed Ryan?"

Trevor's face was inches away from her. "Jana, are you calling me a murderer?"

Backing off, Jana said, "I just asked a question…to try to get to know you better."

He grabbed her shoulder hard. "Here's something to know about me, Jana. Anybody who messes with me eventually regrets it." Trevor released her shoulder. "Tell Gloria I'll see her, and you, tomorrow." And he was gone.

Jana composed herself then went upstairs to Brian Jr.'s room. After Gloria handed him to his mother, Jana sat on the rocking chair and rocked him back and forth, while kissing his soft cheeks. Looking up at the dancing bears and elephants on the wallpaper, Jana said, "Trevor left. He said he'll see you tomorrow."

Gloria changed the blanket in the crib. "Thanks."

"Are you okay?"

Gloria nodded. "Trevor has been really helpful."

"I find that hard to believe, given Trevor's sarcasm and cynicism."

Gloria smiled. "He's just doing that thing."

"It's a *thing* all right." Jana added, "Please don't invite him here when I'm not home."

"Okay." Folding the old blanket, Gloria said, "Brian called when you were at the guest cottage. I told him you were with Jason."

"Terrific." Jana placed Brian Jr. back in his crib.

"Did I do something wrong?"

Jana took a deep breath. "Everything's fine, Gloria. Just take care of yourself…and Brian Jr."

Brian Jr. concurred with, "Fi-fi Glo-a."

That evening, since the master bedroom was still a mess from the film, Jana changed into her teal silk nightgown and decided to sleep in her middle son's bedroom. Being close to her son's things made her miss him less. Sitting on Ed's horse-shaped chair, she picked up her son's cowboy phone, and called Brian. She let out a sigh of relief when Brian answered. *Thank goodness.* "Brian."

"Hi, babe. How was your date with Jason Apollo?"

She raised her eyes to the gallon hat lighting fixture. "We were rehearsing. And it was productive. The scenes we shot today were fine, too."

"I'm glad my girl is doing well. I never had any doubts."

Putting her legs up on the wooden four-poster bed, Jana looked at the ranch pictures on the wallpaper. "How are the malls coming along?"

Brian filled Jana in on his business meetings in Dallas. She in turn told him about Ryan, including his history with women, and her suspicions of Jack, Tom, and Trevor.

Brian's tone of voice conveyed concern. "Jan, promise me you'll be careful, and stay close to Gloria and Brian Jr."

"I will."

"Is Simon coming to watch shooting again tomorrow?"

"I don't think I could keep him away."

"Good. He'll look out for you until I get back."

"When is that?"

"Soon, babe. I promise."

Jana said, "I'm going to keep you to your promise."

"I'm counting on it."

Jana kissed the mouthpiece then hung up the phone. After collapsing onto Ed's bed, she instantly fell asleep.

At three o'clock in the morning, Jana bolted up in bed. *Trevor Masquer is Jack Capello's son!*

Chapter 5

The next morning, Jana fed, changed, and bathed Brian Jr. then changed into her wardrobe for the day—designer jeans and an indigo turtleneck.

Sitting in one of the blue wingback chairs with rose inlay in the upstairs sitting room, Jana enjoyed a private makeup/dish session with Hylas.

Popping part of a candy bar into his mouth, then scratching his bald head, Hylas said, "Girl, we'll need a sandblaster for those bags under your eyes. Didn't you get enough sleep last night?"

As Hylas teased her hair—and teased her—Jana said, "I couldn't stop thinking about what happened yesterday."

"The police lieutenant said it was an accident."

That's the party line.

Hylas popped gum into his mouth. "Don't move." He applied base to her skin and clown white under her eyes. "It couldn't have happened to a nicer guy."

Sitting as still as possible, Jana said, "It was nice of Tom Strong to defend you when Ryan made that homophobic remark."

"Tom is a gentleman. Ryan, excuse my French, was an arrogant pig," Hylas said with a snap of his gum.

Feeling like a gossip columnist, Jana asked, "Why did Tom get so upset when Ryan mentioned Tom's wife? Do you think there was something going on between Mrs. Strong and Ryan O'Halloran?"

"Please. If you were married to Tom Strong, would you have an affair with *Ryan O'Halloran*? Close your eyes." Hylas applied blue eye shadow on Jana's eyelids.

"Then why do you think Tom reacted that way?"

"You know men. They get their backs—and everything else—up quickly."

They shared a laugh.

Hylas continued working on Jana's eyes with eyeliner, an eyebrow pencil, and a mascara wand. "I've worked with Tom on lots of films. He's a real stand-up guy. And not too hard on the eyes either. Speaking of gorgeous guys, did you and Jason rehearse last night?"

"Yes."

"Don't move. You two seem pretty cozy."

"Jason and I are colleagues. Nothing more."

Hylas grinned from ear to ear. "Um, hm." He applied rouge to her cheekbones, and lipstick to her lips. "What's going to happen when hubby gets home?"

"Brian will return to a devoted wife and mother."

"One out of two ain't bad, honey."

Jana made her way downstairs to the great room, where she filled a bowl with yogurt, berries, and granola then sat at the bar.

"Careful not to mess your makeup, baby doll." Simon took the stool next to her. He was wearing a fuchsia and tangelo jumpsuit with a lemon scarf and matching waist pouch.

"Good morning, Simon. Brian wants you to look out for me."

He patted Jana's knee. "I always have, and I always will, baby doll."

Jana smiled. "Thank you, Simon." Jana sat down to eat her breakfast. "We're shooting in the kitchen today."

Simon raised his tiny hands to the cathedral ceiling. "Where will Theresa watch her soap operas?"

Jana giggled. "I gave her the day off."

As if gossiping in a sewing circle, Simon asked, "Is Trevor Masquer upstairs with your nanny?"

"He just arrived in makeup." After a sigh, Jana added, "Gloria will no doubt come down when Trevor is called to the set."

"Isn't Trevor a bit old to need a nanny?"

Jana replied, "I'm certainly not a fan of Trevor's, but he seems to be helping Gloria through a rough time."

"What's wrong? Brian Jr.'s been pooping too much?" Simon asked with a devilish smirk.

"Simon." Jana hit his small shoulder playfully.

As technicians, clerks, and designers raced around them like cars at the Grand Prix, Myrna Buller took the stool on Jana's other side. Wearing skintight gold stretch pants and a silver sweatshirt with gold sequins, Myrna ran a hand through her frizzy red hair, nearly knocking off her tortoise shell glasses. "Let's hope things run more smoothly today, bubalas."

"Amen," said Jana.

Myrna wrapped a cheese pastry inside a napkin, and placed it into her large leopard pocketbook. After adjusting her girdle, she said, "Jack will be extra careful to make sure there are no more accidents on the set."

Pouring herself a glass of cranberry juice, Jana said, "Myrna, speaking of Jack, since you put together the package for this film, you must know quite a lot about him."

Cutting to the chase, Myrna asked, "What do you want to know about him, girlchick?"

"Jack and Trevor Masquer seem to have a…special relationship."

"Of course. They're both my clients," Myrna said proudly.

Jana asked, "Are they related?"

Myrna let out a nasal cackle. "We're all related in the movie business, bubala."

I'm not letting you off the hook that easy, Myrna. "Trevor and I had a talk last night."

Myrna crinkled her tiny nose and her mustache hairs looked like a kick line. "I thought you had dinner with *Jason* last night?"

Simon nearly fell off his stool. "Do tell, baby girl."

Feeling like a prisoner under interrogation, Jana said, "Relax, you two. Jason and I rehearsed over dinner. When I got back from the guest cottage, I found Trevor here with Gloria. And based on some things Trevor told me about his parents, and watching Jack and Trevor on the set, I think Jack is Trevor's father."

Simon said, "Spill the dirt, Myrna. Is it true?"

"Ask Jack and Trevor," Myrna replied with a shrug.

Jana said, "Please tell me, Myrna. I promise to keep whatever you say confidential. Knowing the truth will help me work better with both of them." *And hopefully figure out who killed Ryan O'Halloran.*

After a thoughtful pause, Myrna looked around the room like a terrorist at an airport metal detector. Then she motioned for Jana and Simon to come closer. When they were inches from her face, Myrna whispered,

"Don't breathe a word of this to anyone besides Trevor and Jack. Trevor chose a different stage name, and kept his relationship with Jack a secret, because he doesn't want people to think he was cast in Jack's film due to nepotism."

"Which of course he was," said Simon with a double eye-roll.

"Sh," Myrna continued covertly, "Trevor is a sweet kid."

And I'm Mother Theresa.

"He studied acting very hard, did a year in rep, and he wants to be appreciated for his talents," said Myrna.

"Myrna, I know how fiercely loyal you and Simon are to your clients. I find that admirable. But just for a moment, Myrna, forgetting you are their manager, do you think Jack and Trevor could have had something to do with the light falling on Ryan yesterday?"

Myrna's back went up. "The lieutenant said it was an accident."

Simon looked like a cat with a canary in its mouth. "Maybe it was a *planned* accident."

"That's ridiculous," Myrna said with her jowls flapping like shutters in the wind. "Movie people don't hurt other movie people."

Tell that to Jack's wife.

Myrna scratched her three chins. "*If* Ryan's death was not an accident, I suspect your pastor, bubala."

"He's not *my* pastor," Jana replied, noticing her voice had become shrill.

"Well he's *somebody's* pastor," Myrna said. "That man went on and on about how movie thrillers nowadays are soft core pornography, and *he* was going to put an end to this smut and save all of our mortal souls."

Simon added, "I wished he had saved me a cookie on the dessert tray."

Before Jana could reply, she was called to the set for her next scene.

When Jana entered the kitchen, she cringed at the lights, cables, microphones, monitors, sandbags, and crew people covering every inch of the room. Tools, bags, scripts, and slate boards were stationed on the two islands, glass tabletop, and ceramic floor tiles.

Jack, appearing more relaxed than the day before, asked Jana to take her first position next to the sink.

Trevor Masquer stood next to her. After the slate and call for action, they went through the scene, where Trevor pushed himself on Jana, and Jana fearfully backed away. The two of them had great chemistry, and the scene was exciting and credible.

As the crew people changed lighting, sound, and camera angles for the second take, Trevor said to Jana, "You should loosen up. I don't think your character is *that* frigid."

Is the carpenter's hammer handy? "I'm sure Jack will tell me if I need to make a character adjustment."

Rubbing his wide nose, Trevor replied, "Jack's too nice. Trust me; you need to lighten up, babe."

"Listen, *babe*, since we're in the kitchen...*my* kitchen, let's remember the old metaphor, too many cooks spoil the broth."

"Is there a problem?" Jack rubbed his weather-beaten face.

Trevor grimaced. "Yeah, there's a *problem*. Jana's character should be turned on to me then frightened when I pounce."

Jack replied, "Concentrate on your own role, Trevor, and let Jana play hers, which she is doing just fine by the way."

"But the way Jana is playing her role minimizes mine," said Trevor meeting Jack eye for eye.

"Just play the scene, Trevor," said Jack with a no-nonsense look.

Laughing bitterly, Trevor said, "Is that the best you can do as director?"

Jana put her hand on her hip. "Trevor, it's clear you don't respect *me*, but you need to respect Jack…for the obvious reasons."

Hovering over her, Trevor said, "What are the *obvious* reasons?"

Jana stepped away from him, noticing the wild look in Trevor's dark, deep set eyes. "You know the reasons, Trevor."

He came closer to her. "I asked you a question."

She whispered in his ear, "You shouldn't talk to your director…or your *father* like that."

Coming nose to nose with her, Trevor whispered back, "You're too nosey for your own good, Jana. That might hurt you one day."

Jack called for quiet, slate then yelled, "Action!"

Jana and Trevor did the scene again. Given their heightened emotional state, the scene was quite powerful. The people watching held their breath in anticipation of what would happen next as the energy bounced back and forth between Jana and Trevor like lightning. The scene ended with Trevor storming out of the kitchen, followed by a collective sigh of relief from the spectators, including Simon and Myrna.

While the technicians set up for the next take, Jana

noticed Gloria talking to Trevor in what looked like an attempt to calm him down. He kissed Gloria hard on the mouth then returned for the last take, which was even more intense than the second. Jana and Trevor played the scene like two wrestlers, pushing and pulling in battle. When Jack called, "Cut," Jana was exhausted. Trevor pushed away a technician, and stormed out of the kitchen.

Myrna and Gloria went after Trevor, and Simon rushed over to Jana and held her in his small arms. "You were wonderful. Are you all right, baby doll?"

She rested her head on his tiny shoulder. "I'm glad *that's* over."

"Me, too, baby girl. Come and tell Mama all about it."

While the crew set up for the next scene, Jana cooled off over a glass of lemonade at the great room's bar with Simon. When Myrna and Gloria returned to the great room, minus Trevor, Jana excused herself and walked over to Gloria in a corner of the room.

"Gloria, is Brian Jr. all right?"

She nodded. "He's asleep."

"And are *you* all right?" Jana asked.

"Trevor was upset," Gloria replied.

"I witnessed that firsthand. Are *you* all right, Gloria?"

Gloria's blue eyes softened. "I'm fine, and Trevor cooled down after Myrna and I talked to him."

"Are you sure you want to get involved with this guy?"

Gloria looked like a cultist at the pink lemonade stand. "There's more to Trevor Masquer than you know, Jana."

"That's what I'm afraid of." Jana started to walk away, but stopped herself. "What do you *see* in him?"

Gloria sighed. "Jana, Trevor's smart, talented, and he has a big future."

Not believing the girl's naivety, Jana said, "And you think he'll remember you when this shoot is over and he's back in LA?"

Gloria's eyes brimmed with tears. "Jana, I'm a better judge of character than you think."

"That certainly wasn't the case with Ryan O'Halloran." Jana regretted it the minute the words left her lips.

Gloria looked as if she'd been stabbed in the heart. "I like working here. I really do. The kids are terrific. And I appreciate your concern about me." Gloria dug her heels into the carpet. "I know I've made a lot of mistakes, but I'm not a child. I'm twenty-five years old."

"Of course you're not a child, Gloria."

A production intern stood next to them looking uncomfortable. "Excuse me, Miss Lane. Your pastor is at the front door. He said he needs to discuss some concerns he has about the film with you." The young woman smirked. "And he asked if the film company would like to make a donation to his church."

"Thank you," Jana said to the young woman who ran off to do her next errand. Turning back to Gloria, Jana said, "Please, do me a favor. Tell Rev. Charlton I am working and not able to speak with him. And please remind him this is a closed set." *And I will break one of the Ten Commandments, murder, if he comes here again.*

Gloria nodded then looked over her shoulder for

Trevor as she headed for the front door.

Jana headed for the wardrobe mistress then changed into a button-down cream silk blouse and turquoise skirt with matching shoes, necklace, and earrings.

When Jana arrived back in the great room, she saw Gloria and Trevor heading upstairs. Following them at a safe distance, a technique she learned in *The Girl Detective*, Jana peered around the hallway wall to see Gloria and Trevor enter Gloria's bedroom then shut the door. After making her way to Brian Jr.'s room, Jana checked on her sleeping child. Then using a technique she learned from her spy girl movie, Jana flipped the switch on the intercom resting on the night table. Having changed the intercom's direction, Jana sat on the rocking chair and listened to Gloria and Trevor in Gloria's bedroom.

Trevor said with rage brewing in his voice, "It's a big deal to *me*."

"Why?" Gloria asked.

"Because I don't want to be looked at like some no-talent, snot-nosed, privileged, rich kid whose father put him in the movies. I worked hard to get this break."

"Everyone knows that, and everyone respects your talents, Trevor."

He laughed bitterly. "Right, just like Ryan O'Halloran did."

"What does *he* know?"

"Not much anymore." During what sounded like pacing, Trevor said, "I don't know why she *hates* me. I *tried* to be friends with her."

Gloria replied, "Jana's got a lot on her plate right now. Cut her some slack."

After what sounded like the rustling of clothing, Trevor said, "How about if I don't cut *you* some slack."

Gloria replied, "I'd like that."

Following a kiss, Trevor said, "Jana better not tell anyone about my dad." After another kiss, he added, "You have to help me, Gloria." After another kiss, "Will you do that?"

"I'll help in any way I can, Trevor."

A technician stood in the doorway. "You're needed on set, Miss Lane."

"Thank you, Sam." With thoughts of Nixon's wiretapping sentence the year prior, Jana flipped back the switch on the intercom, and headed downstairs.

Chapter 6

When Jana arrived on the kitchen set, she found Jason Apollo looking fetching in a tight amaranth polo shirt, chestnut khaki slacks, and brown loafers.

As they stood on their first mark, next to the kitchen fireplace, Jason said, "You look terrific."

"Right back at you," Jana replied with a warm smile.

"Myrna told me Trevor gave you a rough time earlier."

Jana whispered, "I'm more hopeful about this scene."

He winked. "I'll go easy on you."

After Hylas touched up their makeup, pronouncing them both, "absolutely gorgeous," Jack called for the first take.

Jana and Jason executed the scene smoothly. Jason's competence as a detective and growing affection for Jana were palpable in the scene. It was also quite clear that Jana, though distraught about the death of her husband and emotional state of her Guy Friday, was falling hard and fast for Jason.

Is art imitating life, or am I a better actress than I thought.

The next two takes were even better. When they were through, Jack called for lunch.

Jana and Jason made their plates at the great room

bar then escaped the chaos by eating in the sun porch. Upon sitting on the white wicker rocking chairs, they looked through the glass wall to the acres of shiny green grass, sparkling blue river, and jagged brown mountains in the distance.

Digging into his chicken Caesar salad, Jason said, "What an amazing day. Too bad we aren't shooting outside."

Jana speared a broccoli from her broccoli, kale, cauliflower, cranberry salad. "Rumor has it we're shooting at the flower garden tomorrow." *There go my beautiful flowers.*

Looking like a kid asking for a new bicycle, Jason looked out at Jana's swimming pool. "Is it all right if I use your pool tonight?"

"Of course."

"I don't want to impede on your privacy."

With a pointed glance at the horde of people scurrying around outside the doorway, Jana replied, "Yes, I have so much privacy."

They shared a laugh.

Jason took a sip of milk, rested it on the glass top of the white wicker end table, and flicked back his thick blond hair.

He's still the boy from Kentucky.

"Do you want me to talk to Trevor Masquer about his behavior with you today?" Jason asked, ready to assume the role of knight in shining armor.

Jana sipped her cranberry juice. "I can handle Trevor." She looked off, deep in thought. "I hope Gloria can, too."

"Ah, a movie romance." Jason's blue eyes sparkled under the Tiffany chandelier. "Happens all the time."

Jana looked at her wedding ring and reminded herself of her wedding vows. "I'm sure it happens to you frequently."

He replied, "Actually, it doesn't."

"I'm sorry if I was out of bounds."

"You weren't."

"Well, I certainly was with Gloria. I think I offended her." Jana bit her lip. "I can't help worrying about the girl."

"She looks all grown up to me."

"That's what *she* said, but looks can be deceiving." Jana rested her plate on the end table and tented her fingers. "Outside, Gloria is obviously an adult. But inside, she's a girl who believes the film business is a panacea, a perfect fantasy world that will solve all her problems."

Jason released his amazing dimples. "Isn't it?"

Jana said, "I worry about young people who want so desperately to be in show business, they'll do almost anything to join the ranks. The ones who don't make it feel deficient and worthless. The ones who finally do realize not a great deal has changed in their lives. They still have the same problems they had before."

"Hopefully they live and learn."

I can't believe how easy it is to talk to you. "What would you have done if Myrna didn't discover you playing Romeo back in Kentucky?"

"Probably work in the coal mining business like my father."

"Would you have been happy?"

"I don't think so."

"But doesn't happiness come from within? Can't a coal miner be as content as a movie star, and a movie star be as miserable as a coal miner?"

"Of course. It's about being true to yourself...to who you really are inside."

"Exactly. My father was in show business. It was natural for me. I never needed it to exist. I wasn't foolish enough to think being an actress would take away all of my problems."

He stretched back in his chair. "And what *are* your problems, Jana Lane?"

I'm very happily married and at the same time magnetically attracted to you. "Like most women nowadays, including I assume Sandra Day O'Connor, I watch myself getting older, and when I look in the mirror, I don't always like who stares back."

He looked clear through to her soul. "I like what I see, Jana. And I like who you are. You should, too. It took me a long time to like myself, and it's much better than hating yourself, trust me."

Jana's eyes doubled in size. "*You* didn't like yourself?"

"I wanted to crawl out of my skin when I was a kid. I owe Myrna a great deal. She helped me find myself, and become the man I am today."

The result is certainly amazing. Changing the subject before she lost control, Jana asked, "How do you think the film is going so far?"

"Fine. I'd make another film with Jana Lane in a heartbeat."

"Me, too." *That didn't come out right.*

"Two Jana Lanes in one film? Didn't you do that in one of your old movies?"

"I did, didn't I?"

They giggled.

Jana said, "Shooting out of sequence is a bit confusing on the emotions. I mourned my dead husband yesterday, and I'm doing a scene with Tom in the kitchen this afternoon."

She put her drink down on the end table at the same time he lifted his, and their hands touched. Jason took Jana's hand in his. It felt warm, inviting, and completely natural.

He said, "I feel like we're an old married couple, sitting on the sun porch waiting for the sun to go down."

"Brian and I haven't gotten to that point yet. Devon, Ed, and Brian Jr. keep us hopping." *Maybe if I talk about my family, I'll remember I have one.*

Jason squeezed her hand. "Brian is a lucky man."

"*I'm* the lucky one."

"Of course you are." He winked. "You're having lunch with Jason Apollo."

She threw her napkin at him. "As created by Myrna Buller."

He laughed. "Your manager and my agent seem to be getting along well."

"So I noticed."

"Could romance be blossoming?" Jason asked tongue firmly in cheek.

Jana laughed. "There's about as much chance of that happening as Arnold Schwarzenegger the bodybuilder becoming governor."

"Does Simon have anyone in his life—" He pinched her chin. "—besides you?"

Jana finished the last few bites of her lunch before replying, "Simon and Jonas were together for many many years, until Jonas passed away from a stroke. I'm working on a fundraiser for AIDS at the Vanderbilt museum with Simon's current boyfriend, Cornelius. He's a musician." She grimaced. "*Boyfriend*, what a strange word for two elderly, committed people. Do you think gay couples will ever be able to get married?"

He shook his head no. "I can't imagine it." Then, scraping his plate, Jason said, "You're very brave...doing the AIDS fundraiser."

Jana's jaw dropped. "What's so brave about raising money for people in need?"

He squirmed in his white wicker seat. "No other celebrity will touch it. It's a total stigma. The politicians and church leaders won't even talk about it."

Like a bull seeing a red cape of bigotry, Jana said, "The brave souls are the victims of this dreaded plague. Ignoring them in their sickness and death is inhuman. Our elected officials and so-called religious leaders should hang their heads in shame."

"Your pastor wouldn't agree with you."

Jana slammed her plate down on the glass tabletop. "Reverend Rodney Charlton is *not* my pastor. He's a self-serving, bullying parasite who is determined to close down this film and stop the AIDS fundraiser."

Putting his hand on her knee, Jason said, "Then we'll just have to stop him."

Jana caught her breath. "We'll?"

"Do you want another celebrity for your fundraiser?"

"Will Myrna let you do that?"

"It's not her decision."

She happily threw her arms around his massive neck. "Thank you, Jason."

Myrna stood at the doorway, watching Jana and

Jason in mid-embrace. She cleared her throat, and they parted. Then Myrna patted one of the rolls of fat under her girdle. "I didn't mean to interrupt your...whatever you were doing, bubalas, but my tummy is a bit sour."

No doubt from eating at the buffet table all day.

"Jana, bubala, do you have anything to settle my stomach?"

How about a sandblaster? "Of course. I've got something in my bathroom upstairs." Jana hurried off.

Upon reaching the top of the spiral staircase, Jana heard voices from the makeup room. She paused near the doorway when she realized Tom Strong and Hylas were engaged in what sounded like a heated argument—about *her*.

Hylas said, "I think you can trust Jana."

"I don't," Tom replied, clearly agitated.

"So you're going to jeopardize her life?"

"I am *not* going to *jeopardize* everything I've worked so long and hard to get!"

As Tom stormed out of the makeup room, Jana made a beeline for her bedroom. After retrieving the stomach medicine, she headed back downstairs and offered it to Myrna who was eating a bowl of ice cream at the great room bar.

Myrna rubbed one of her stomach rolls. "I hear ice cream is good for the digestion."

Handing her the bottle, Jana said, "I hope this helps."

Myrna accepted it like a trophy from her gymnastic days. "Thank you, bubala. You are a lifesaver." She opened the bottle and drank from it. "Here, sit, sit."

Jana sat next to her.

"I couldn't help but notice you and Jason on the

sun porch. So, tell me. What's going on with you two bubalas? Should I tell the PR people to promote the movie—and your engagement?"

"I'm not a bigamist, Myrna." *Just a wife and mother feeling guilty.*

After a loud belch, Myrna said like a TV talk show host desperate for high ratings, "Are you sure there's nothing between you two?"

Simon put his arm around Jana. "My baby doll is faithful to her hubby, who by the way is not so shabby in the looks department either." He whispered as if mentioning a terminal illness, "Though Brian isn't in show business." He added with a gleam in his eyes, "And the coupling of Jana Lane and Jason Apollo would be big news."

Feeling as uncomfortable as a turkey in November, Jana said, "I'll let you two debate my personal life, while I change for the next scene."

Jana took her next outfit off the costume rack, and changed in the downstairs powder room.

Entering the kitchen, wearing a jade fleece shirt and matching slacks, Jana took her opening spot at one of the two sinks.

Hylas shouted, "Emergency hair repair!" and touched up her hair and makeup.

Since the scene was from early in the film, it was a warm, touching one, where Jana sends her husband, the governor, off to work with a kiss. In thrillers, it is called the calm before the storm scene. Tom stood next to her, in his designer cobalt three-piece suit, waiting for Jack to call for slate and action. Jana couldn't help notice how tired and drawn he looked. *I wonder if it's because of his argument on the phone with his wife, or his argument with Hylas in the makeup room—about me.*

While a technician refocused a light, Jana asked Tom, "Is everything okay?"

"Sure," he replied with a warm smile. "Something wrong?"

"You look tired."

He raised his eyes to the boom microphone. "Probably from the lumpy bed in the hotel."

But you said your hotel room was very comfortable. "Tom, is everything all right between us?"

"Of course. You're my loving wife."

They shared a smile.

Jana touched his hand. "If I did anything to offend you, you'd tell me?"

"You couldn't offend anyone." He squeezed her hand. "You're Jana Lane, everyone's best friend."

A sound technician called for time out while he changed a sound level.

Back to the investigation. "I'm still a bit shaken about what happened to Ryan O'Halloran."

"I think we *all* are, especially the lighting crew."

"Tom, did you know Ryan well?"

He shrugged his large shoulders. "I worked with him on a couple of film shoots."

She rested a hand on his thick forearm. "Does your wife ever come and watch your scenes?"

After a laugh, he replied, "Never."

"I thought someone mentioned you and your wife were close friends of Ryan's." *Was that subtle enough?*

"My wife and Ryan's ex-wife were friends." Tom rubbed his neck uncomfortably.

Jana came closer and whispered, "Tom, please tell me if this is none of my business, but was Ryan the reason you were arguing with your wife?"

His eyes widened. "Jana, if you're asking if Ryan and my wife had an affair, the honest answer is, I don't know."

Jack called for quiet, slate, and "Action!"

The scene went well on each take with Jana and Tom quite believable as loving husband and wife. Unlike her sizzling onscreen kiss with Jason, Tom kissed her anemically as a sign of affection between a longtime couple whose love had shifted from passionate to comfortable.

At the end of the day, Jana couldn't wait to wash her face, tie her hair back, change into a sweatshirt and jeans, check on Brian Jr., call Devon and Ed, and speak to Brian.

"I don't like this, Jana." Brian's voice carried hints of exhaustion.

Lying on the gold-trimmed chaise in their bedroom, Jana replied, "I'm perfectly safe."

"With a punk young actor and a macho older actor threatening you?"

"They didn't *threaten* me."

After a long exhale, Brian said, "I knew this was a bad idea."

Rubbing the sides of her temples, Jana replied, "You said I should do the movie."

"Because I knew you wanted to do it. I was against it from the start."

"Thank you for being honest with me, Brian!"

"Thank *you* for offering Jason Apollo our guest cottage without asking me!"

"You weren't here!" *I can empathize with Tom feeling tired after arguing with his wife on the phone.*

Jana closed her burning eyes. "I don't want to fight."

Brian sounded like a kid with a stolen candy. "Me either."

Holding her breath, Jana asked, "Brian, when are you coming home?" *Please say tomorrow.*

After a long pause, Brian said, "There's a problem."

No.

"Some of our designs have been kicked back by corporate, and we have to redo them. Of course that will stall construction."

I want you home.

"We're trying to move as quickly as possible. With so many people breathing down my neck, I feel like I'm in a wind tunnel. I want this to work. For *us*."

"So your work is for *us*, and my work is for *me*?"

"I thought we weren't fighting."

She giggled in spite of herself. "I miss you."

"I miss you, too, babe." After a rustling noise, Brian said, "I better get back to work on these designs before I konk out for the night. Promise me you'll take care of yourself?"

"I promise."

"And stay close to Simon and Gloria."

"I will."

Brian swallowed hard. "And give my son a big hug and kiss for me."

"Done."

"You still love me, babe?"

"More than life itself."

Jana hung up then wept into the white provincial phone. Hearing the doorbell chime, Jana wiped her eyes with the sleeve of her sweatshirt, returned the Jana Lane porcelain doll from her walk-in closet to the top of the dresser, and headed down the spiral stairs.

Jana opened the heavy door to a middle-aged, heavy-set couple with painted smiles on their faces. The man wore a drab gray business suit, and the woman had on an equally drab brown dress.

He said, "Hello, Mrs. Otley. I hope you remember us? Mr. and Mrs. Blanley from the town hall meetings?"

Opening the door wider, Jana replied, "Of course, Mr. and Mrs. Blanley. Please come in."

Making their way to the front hallway, Mrs. Blanley said obsequiously, "We don't want to bother you, Mrs. Otley."

"Please, call me, Jana." *What are their first names again?* "Won't you come into the white sitting room?"

Mrs. Blanley started forward, but Mr. Blanley grasped her arm to keep her in place.

A line appeared on Jana's forehead. "Is there a problem?"

Mr. Blanley rubbed his lower jowl. "I'm afraid there is."

"We didn't make a fuss when vans full of equipment drove in and out of your property," Mrs. Blanley said with a pious nod. "What you do in your own home is your business."

How kind of you.

Mr. Blanley scratched the comb-over hair on the top of his head. "But this other thing is another matter entirely."

Standing under the prism chandelier hanging from the cathedral ceiling, Jana felt as if on trial for war crimes. "Are you sure you wouldn't like to sit down?"

Mr. Blanley shook his head and his pudgy cheeks fluttered, making him look like a cartoon character. "Mrs. Otley, we attend The Only Way to Heaven Church, and we watch Reverend Charlton's cable television show each week. Last Sunday, Reverend Charlton's sermon had us quite startled."

I'm not surprised.

Mrs. Blanley fidgeted with the string of pearls around her neck. "Some of the congregants are upset about your movie. We feel if they don't like the content, they don't have to go see it."

"But this other matter affects every one of us," Mr. Blanley said like a judge at the Salem witch trials. "We can't stand idly by while you bring the homosexual lifestyle and their dreaded disease into our community."

Not sure if the fire in her face was from the sunlight shining through the overhead skylights or her rising blood pressure, Jana replied, "And just what is the *homosexual lifestyle*, Mr. Blanley, and how am I bringing *disease* into our community?"

A solemn look filled his pasty face. "Mrs. Otley, the Lord is quite clear about the dangers of promiscuity."

And he told you this?

"We are good, hardworking, honest people. We don't hate anyone, or want to see anyone hurt."

You could have fooled me.

"But we must be practical. There is no cure for this disease. The doctors don't fully know how it is transmitted. Reverend Charlton believes it is God's wrath against a lifestyle that is immoral and unpleasing to the Lord. Like the people of Sodom and Gomorrah, if we sit idly by and do nothing, we might all succumb to this dreaded disease and perish!"

Mrs. Blanley nodded like a doll with a wire neck.

It's time to stop the insanity. "Mr. and Mrs. Blanley, there is no *homosexual lifestyle* just like there is no *heterosexual lifestyle*. Most gay people work, have homes, have partners, and lead lives similar to yours and mine. Gay people are already a part of our community. Unlike in Africa where this dreaded disease has hit mostly heterosexuals, for some reason, this plague in our country has hit more gay men than we can count."

"Due to their promiscuity!"

Jana took in a deep breath. "Is it any wonder that some gay men who have been told they are immoral, cannot marry, and must remain in the shadows have resorted to backroom behavior?" Before he could reply, Jana continued. "And the story of Sodom and Gomorrah was about greed and rape, *not* same-sex love."

"Not according to Reverend Charlton," Mrs. Blanley said, like a grade school teacher giving a student a failing grade.

Why did I answer the door? "Mr. and Mrs. Blanley, the medical establishment is relatively sure this disease is not transmitted through casual contact. My event for AIDS at the Vanderbilt mansion is for *fundraising*. Hopefully we can raise enough money to make a dent in the research and treatment money that is so severely needed to fight this disease."

"Reverend Charlton has asked each of us to do our part to stop you and your...event," explained Mr. Blanley.

Jana's back stiffened. "And just what is Reverend

Charlton's flock going to do?"

Mrs. Blanley placed her perfume-stained hand on Jana's shoulder. "Mrs. Otley, I enjoyed your movies so much when I was a girl."

"And you seemed like a nice lady at the town hall meetings," Mr. Blanley added. "That's why we came here to ask you to please cancel your event. If you don't, a lot of people will be fighting you on this."

Shaking her arm free, Jana asked, "And how exactly will they be *fighting me*?"

Mr. Blanley replied, "As Christian soldiers with the power of the Lord on *our* side. It is our freedom of religion to stand in your way of supporting these...lepers."

Didn't Jesus minister to the outcasts? "*My* religion has taught me to help others in need. And that is what I plan to do. Please feel free to spread the word to your followers."

Mr. Blanley answered, "I hope you don't regret that, Mrs. Otley."

"Is that a threat, Mr. Blanley?"

The doorbell rang.

Jana yanked the heavy wooden door open to reveal Jason Apollo, wearing an aqua terrycloth robe and flip-flips. "I apologize if I'm interrupting something."

No apologies necessary. "Jason, please come in."

As Jason stood next to Mrs. Blanley, her body quivered. "Excuse me, are you Jason Apollo?"

"Yes."

Mrs. Blanley opened her purse and turned away from him. After quickly applying lipstick, she faced Jason and displayed a painted red smile. "I'm a big fan of yours. I've seen all your movies."

Jason smiled and extended his thick hand. "Jason Apollo."

Giggling like a schoolgirl at the gluing station in art class, she placed her hand in his. "It's so nice to meet you, Mr. Apollo. I'm Joyce."

"Mrs. Frank Blanley," Mr. Blanley said, obviously disapproving of his wife's newfound friend.

Not releasing Jason's hand, Mrs. Blanley asked, "How do you like Hyde Park, Mr. Apollo?"

He looked at Jana. "I love it."

Mrs. Blanley cooed like a newborn. "I'm so glad. How long will you be staying?"

"At least until our film is shot."

Mrs. Blanley batted her eyelashes. "Mr. Apollo—"

"Please, call me Jason."

She giggled. "All right, Jason, would you do us the honor of coming to our home for dinner some evening?"

"Well, I—"

Faster than Reverend Charlton's pitch for money on his cable television show, Mrs. Blanley said, "Tomorrow night?"

Mr. Blanley put his arm around his wife and ushered her out the door. "We will be in touch, Mr. Apollo." He locked eyes with Jana. "Please think about what we said, Mrs. Otley. These are very trying times."

We agree there.

Jana shut the door and rested her back against it.

"I take it that wasn't a social call," Jason said.

"Mrs. Blanley sure wanted to get *social* with you."

"She has good taste, what can I say?" Running his hand through his thick blond hair, Jason asked, "Care to join me for a swim?"

Resting her elbow against the door, Jana said, "If you said that on our local television station, every woman in the Hudson Valley would be lined up at my front door."

His eyes glistened in the light from the stained-glass window. "I don't want to go swimming with every woman in the Hudson Valley. Even *your* pool isn't *that* large. I'd like to go swimming with *you*."

To Jana's surprise, she burst out into a fit of laughter.

"I guess my next movie should be a comedy."

She waved her hands then used them to wipe the tears off her cheeks. "It's been a long day."

"All the more reason you should take a relaxing dip in the pool." His boyish dimples appeared.

After a pause, Jana shrugged her shoulders. "Why not? Maybe swimming will stop me from wanting to drown my neighbors."

He replied, "Then again, maybe I prefer swimming alone."

She pushed him away playfully. As she headed up the stairs, Jana said, "Please go out back and make yourself at home. There are towels and floats in the cabana, along with who knows what else Devon and Ed stuffed in there when I wasn't looking.

Five minutes later, Jana entered the pool area in a raspberry one-piece bathing suit and matching swim jacket. She placed a tray of lemonade on a small table. As she threw her jacket on a chaise lounge, she noticed Jason doing laps in her heart-shaped pool.

After finishing his last lap, Jason hoisted himself out of the water and stood next to Jana.

It's like looking at the statue of David in Florence.

Jana's knees buckled at the site of the water droplets falling from Jason's powerful shoulders, high-peaked pectoral muscles, rounded biceps, ripped abdominals, sculpted thighs, and powerful calves. Filling every inch of his aqua Speedos, Jason offered his hand. "Join me. It's nice and warm."

It's warm all right.

Jana and Jason dove in and enjoyed a swim as the sun's rays surrounded them like spinning golden thread. Before feeling waterlogged, they used the ladder to step out. After toweling off, they lay on chaise lounges staring out at the shimmering Hudson River and majestic mountain range in the distance. Then Jana and Jason drank their lemonade and basked in the warmth of the sun.

Jason put on a pair of stylish sunglasses from his robe pocket. "What are you thinking, Jana Lane?"

How amazing you look in those sunglasses. "Do you really want to know?"

"I really want to know."

She sighed. "This has been the most frustrating day."

He sat up on the chaise. "I thought shooting went really well."

"Shooting was fine. The rest of the day was like going to war."

"Want to tell me about it?"

For some reason I do. "You sure you want to hear my problems?"

Jason said in a southern dialect, "Let's pretend we're back on my little front porch in Kentucky. You just came over for some lemonade. While the kids play in our backyard, you tell me what ails you, honey."

She was impressed. "You've done an amazing job changing your speech."

He shook his head no. "The accolades go to Myrna, or rather to her vocal coach."

"Still, it must have been difficult for you, leaving everyone you loved, and everything you knew, coming to Hollywood."

"It wasn't difficult. It was heaven."

The results are certainly out of this world.

His teeth glistened in the sun. "But I thought we were talking about your day, not my Hollywood makeover."

Jana filled Jason in on her threats from Trevor Masquer, Gloria, Tom Strong, and of course the Blanleys. She also told him about her phone conversation with Brian.

Pressing his strong back against the chaise, Jason said, "Okay, Nora, here's how Nick sees things. Trevor Masquer is a spoiled brat. Gloria is attracted to him because of her low self-esteem and the movie dust in her young eyes. Tom Strong is a standup guy. He was probably in a bad mood because of the argument he had with his wife. The Blanleys are totally ridiculous. Why do people think their religious beliefs give them the right to tell other people how to live...or not to live?" He exhaled. "I guess that's how most wars were started."

"It seems Reverend Charlton and the Blanleys want to start a war with *me*." Jana sighed. "I wonder if any of them were at war with Ryan O'Halloran?"

"I can't tell you who, if anyone, killed Ryan O'Halloran. Can I still be your first lieutenant?"

She took in his handsome, boyish face and smiled.

"You can be my knight in shining armor."

To her surprise, Jason leaned over and kissed her on the lips. It felt warm, soft, and completely natural.

"What was *that* for?" she asked in shock.

He winked. "You looked like you needed a kiss."

"Jason, I'm a married woman with three children."

He shrugged his shapely shoulders. "We kissed in our scene for the film."

She slid forward on her chaise. "That was acting. This is real life."

"As they say, art imitates life."

"Not *my* life. Even as a kid I understood my movies and my real life were two separate things."

He smirked. "So you really didn't save little Timmy from that shark, those pirates, and that earthquake?"

She slapped his knee playfully. "Jason, I like you."

"I like you, too."

"Unlike with most men, when we're together I feel...comfortable. And I hope after the film wraps we will stay friends."

"We will."

"But that's all we can be...friends." She stared into his trusting eyes. "You are the perfect man. Every woman in America knows that...even Joyce Blanley. But the perfect man for *me* is Brian."

"Your last phone conversation with him didn't sound like it."

Taking his hand, Jana replied, "Jason, all marriages go through highs and lows. Right now Brian and are going through a bit of a bumpy road, but we'll come back into a sunny green meadow soon."

"Jana, I had a rough childhood. I didn't fit in with

the other kids in my school. They teased and even taunted me."

"Why?"

He looked away. "I was short, big-boned, awkward, insecure."

I can't believe that.

"I was a total loner. I didn't fit in with the boys talking about their girlfriends or the girls talking about boyfriends. I'd go to bed each night praying God would take me in my sleep. If it hadn't been for my English teacher casting me as Romeo, I don't know if I would have made it through high school." His aqua eyes glowed.

"When Myrna brought me to Hollywood, everybody treated me like a freak. Even after the makeover, people were distrustful. I had a lot of work to do catching up to other actors, and eventually surpassing them." He unleashed a melancholy smile. "That old expression, you can't go home again is true. When I went back home, I was like an alien. I made everyone uncomfortable, including my own parents...including me. I knew I could never live there again."

He squeezed her hand. "Jana, growing up, I never trusted anybody. Even now, the women you read about in the tabloids are women I've...dated, but I didn't trust. I didn't matter much to any of them. I was a trophy." He hung his head. "And to be honest, they didn't mean much to me either." He put their joined hands over his heart. "I know we've only known each other a short while, but I feel connected to you, like you somehow see the real me inside the fabricated package. I know you're married to Brian, and you have three adorable kids." He looked around. "And all of this. But please, don't shut yourself off to the possibility of getting closer to me. After all we've been through, I think we both deserve it. And I'm pretty sure you want it as much as I do."

Hearing a noise, Jana looked up and saw Gloria watching them for her bedroom balcony. Jason followed Jana's gaze, and Gloria rushed back inside her bedroom.

"Should I take off?" Jason asked, clearly not wanting to leave.

"No, I'll speak with Gloria later."

After they rested in the sun a bit longer, Jason sounded like a commercial for sunscreen. "With your fair skin, you don't want to burn. It can happen quickly. Trust me, I know from my last shoot at the beach. Can I put some suntan lotion on you?"

"Sure. It's in the cabana."

With Jason rummaging through the cabana, Jana rose and looked up at Gloria's bedroom window. Suddenly, feeling a push against her side, Jana slipped into the pool. Remembering a safety move she learned in *Surfer Girl*, when falling in mid air Jana tucked her head into her arms and hit the water in the fetal position. Once in the water, she spun her body around and swam out.

When they returned to their lounges, Jason noticed Jana was wet and out of breath. "Are you all right?"

Wiping herself with the towel he handed her, Jana replied, "It felt like somebody pushed me into the pool."

Jason looked around. "I don't see anyone."

She shrugged her shoulders. "I was looking up at

Gloria's window. Maybe I lost my balance and slipped."

"I better keep a closer watch on you. I don't want to lose my leading lady."

"At least not until we finish shooting."

"Or ever. Here. Turn your back toward me." Sliding to the edge of his lounge chair, Jason applied the sunscreen to Jana's back. It felt warm and luxurious. "My turn."

Jason offered his back, and Jana rubbed lotion on Jason's v-shaped back. Her fingers enjoyed caressing layer after layer of perfectly sculpted muscle until the lotion disappeared into his smooth, tight skin. He seemed to enjoy it, too.

Putting his muscular arms around her and leaning her back into his inviting chest, Jason said, "Let's stay like this forever."

Enjoying Jason's embrace far too much, Jana leapt to her feet. "I better make sure Brian Jr. is all right."

He looked concerned. "Let me know if you need me."

"I'm fine." Jana grabbed her swimming jacket, and went through her kitchen French doors, up the back stairs to Brian Jr.'s room. She found him sleeping soundly in his crib. After kissing his cheek and covering him with his blanky, she looked down the hall and noticed Gloria standing in her bedroom doorway, wearing a pink nightie.

Looking down at the carpet, and sounding like a child of divorce, Gloria asked, "Is something going on between you and Jason Apollo?"

Jana walked over to Gloria and lifted her chin. "Nothing more than mutual admiration and support.

Okay?"

Gloria nodded. "Okay."

"And how about you and Trevor?"

"Jana, you've misjudged Trevor. He's a wonderful guy. Please give him another chance."

"I think I've given him enough chances." Putting her arm around Gloria, Jana said, "Gloria, please don't be too disappointed if you don't see Trevor after the film wraps."

Gloria stared into Jana's eyes. "And please don't be too disappointed if you don't see Jason Apollo."

Jana laughed. After wishing Gloria goodnight, Jana started down the spiral staircase. She noticed something toward the center of the staircase. Reaching the middle step, she screamed at the sight of the porcelain Jana Lane doll with its head severed from its body, and blood dripping down its neck. Jana reached out a shaky hand for the note in the doll's hand, *You're next, Jana.*

Chapter 7

That evening, Jana, Jason, Gloria, and Lieutenant Rivera were in the hunter green and pale peach sitting room.

Standing at the marble fireplace below the antique wall mirror, Rivera ran a strong hand through his black tightly-curled hair, unleashing a windstorm of dandruff onto his black suit jacket. "We dusted. There were no fingerprints on the doll, or on the note."

"But somebody put them on the staircase," Jason said, still in his terrycloth robe, sitting next to Jana on the overstuffed peach loveseat.

Rivera grimaced. "With the amount of people coming and going from this house today, anyone could have put that doll on your staircase, Mrs. Otley."

In a pink robe, Gloria squirmed on the green wingback chair opposite the loveseat. "It wasn't there when I went up to my bedroom."

"When was that?" The lieutenant took a notepad and pencil from his jacket pocket.

After thinking a moment, Gloria replied, "About seven-thirty."

"It wasn't there when I spoke with the Blanleys just before that time," Jana added as she tightened the belt of her swim jacket.

Making a note then closing his pad, Rivera said, "Mrs. Otley, my assumption is this was a practical joke or prank by someone on your film crew."

My assumption is that you are an idiot. "Lieutenant Rivera, after the film crew left, while Jason and I were in the pool and Gloria was in her bedroom, roughly between seven-thirty and eight, someone broke into my home, walked up to my bedroom, took my Jana Lane doll off my dresser, ripped off its head, applied red paint to its neck, and left it on my front staircase with a note telling me I will be next, and you think that is a *harmless prank?*"

Rivera rested an elbow on the cherry wood fireplace mantel. "Mrs. Otley, is your husband still away?"

"Yes."

"And why was Mr. Apollo here this evening?"

Jana felt steam ready to shoot out of her ears. "Jason and I are working on the film together. He's staying in the guest cottage. We went for a swim after shooting."

Smirking, Rivera replied, "Mr. Apollo is a...matinee idol. Perhaps a local fan was jealous of your...relationship."

Rising, Jana said, "Whatever the scenario, someone entered my home with my young child asleep upstairs and threatened me! I also felt someone push me into the pool this evening."

Rivera turned to Gloria. "Did you see anyone besides Mrs. Otley and Mr. Apollo at the pool area?"

Gloria shook her head no.

Looking at Jana like a resident of a mental ward, Rivera said, "Are you sure it wasn't the wind?"

Jana replied bitterly, "You said that once before when I was attacked in the pool."

Nodding, Rivera replied, "Were all the doors locked? Was your security system working?"

Jana nearly fell back onto the loveseat. "I was upset after the Blanleys left. I forgot to lock the front door." She put her head in her hands. "And I left the backdoor open when Jason and I went swimming." *Brian, you always reminded me to lock the doors and put on the alarm.*

Smiling condescendingly, Rivera said, "As I understand it, everyone on your film crew is staying at local hotels. It wouldn't have been difficult for any of them to reenter your home this evening." He sighed. "That's one of the problems with opening your home to a film production company."

Jason put his arm around Jana. "Lieutenant, it's not fair to blame the victim. Jana's property was violated."

"I'll file a report, and my staff will keep a watch on the property," said Rivera.

"That's it?" asked Jason.

Rivera replied, "With nobody hurt and no permanent damage to the premises, that's the best I can do. Mrs. Otley, if the doll is insured, I would contact the insurance company."

With tears brimming in her eyes, Jana replied, "The doll is thirty years old. My old studio sold thousands of them. That was the only one I had."

"As I recall you still have your sister's Jana Lane paper doll books," Rivera said with feigned concern. "I would insure them. I will be in touch if I have any news."

Jana stood and blocked him from exiting the room. "Lieutenant Rivera, there have been a number of suspicious incidents while we were filming. I believe they have something to do with Ryan O'Halloran's death."

Dropping his shoulders and cocking his head to one side, Rivera replied, "Mrs. Otley, I spoke to numerous individuals, and I thoroughly examined and investigated your set. Mr. O'Halloran's death was accidental."

Jana held her ground. "I think you're wrong."

Sounding like a parent telling a child fairies aren't real, Rivera said, "Mrs. Otley, this isn't a movie. It's real life."

I thought it was a nightmare.

"I have many years experience in examining crime scenes. And your home is not one."

It will be after I clobber you.

Jason rose and stood next to Jana. "Lieutenant, won't you at least hear what Jana has to say? It might help your investigation."

Rivera sighed and sat on the wingback chair next to Gloria's. "All right, Mrs. Otley. Play girl detective like you did when you were ten years old."

Standing over him like a lioness ready to pounce, Jana said, "Why do you assume that because I am an actress every word out of my mouth is fakery?"

Rivera rubbed his red eyes. "Mrs. Otley, most people believe police work is like what they see in movies and on television. They don't realize what your industry produces is complete fabrication. Detectives rarely chase after criminals. We hardly ever sit in a room and use *the little gray cells* to figure out *who done it*. What we do is carefully examine and test evidence, weigh the facts then fill out the reports."

Taking Jana's side, literally and figuratively, Jason

said, "And isn't an important part of those things listening to what people have seen and heard?"

Jana added, "I remember when I told you I saw shadows in my basement, and that a car ran me off the road. In both cases you didn't believe me, and both times I was indeed in harm's way."

After a long exhale, he said, "I'm listening, Mrs. Otley."

Jana returned to the loveseat. Jason sat next to her for support.

Say it unemotionally, clearly, and concisely. "Rev. Charlton and his followers are angry with me for hosting an upcoming AIDS fundraising benefit at the Vanderbilt historic estate. I overheard one of my co-stars on this film, Tom Strong, tell our makeup man he doesn't trust me. My other co-star, Trevor Masquer, threatened me on the set today."

Rivera perked up. "How did he threaten you?"

"He told me I was too nosey for my own good, and it might hurt me one day."

"Good advice." Rivera rose. "Mrs. Otley, I will speak with your co-workers again, as well as with Rev. Charlton. In the meantime, please lock your doors, and put on your alarm system in the evenings. I can find my way out." He added with a sarcastic grin, "I'm getting to know this house quite well."

After checking in on Brian Jr., and seeing Gloria off to bed, Jana stood on the upper landing with Jason. "Thank you for standing by me this evening."

"My pleasure." He took her hand. "Can I bring you up some warm milk?"

"I'll be fine after a good cry."

He loosened the belt of his robe. "My chest is

available."

She laughed in spite of herself. "I'll take a rain check."

"You want to call Brian?"

She shook her still wet head. "He'll be asleep by now. I'll call him tomorrow."

Running his smooth finger across her cheek, Jason said, "Would you like me to stay here tonight?"

"Yes, but I don't think that's a very good idea." She walked him down the stairs. "Go back to the cottage, go over your lines, and get some rest. We have a full day of shooting again tomorrow."

"Call me if you need me?"

"Of course."

As they stood in the entrance hallway, Jana thought about the Blanleys. Suddenly, she threw her arms around Jason's shoulders and hugged him tightly. He returned the embrace. Jana wasn't sure how long they held one another.

After they separated, Jason said, "Lock the doors, and put on the alarm."

"I will. Thank you, Jason."

His eyes were full of love and devotion. "We'll get through this, Jana."

She nodded, closed the door, locked it, and turned on the alarm. *I remembered, Brian.* Then Jana went upstairs to her bedroom, where she cried herself to sleep.

****

Jana Lane ran through the woods on her property, out of breath, frightened, feeling totally alone. The footsteps behind her grew louder. A twig snapped beneath her foot. A branch grazed her cheek. Leaves entwined in her hair. She was out of breath. Her legs ached. She had to keep going, keep trying to get away. But from what? A hand reached out. She dodged it. It reached out again. Jana Lane screamed a harrowing shriek...

As if astral projecting from her body, Jana leaped up in bed. Her eyes rapidly cased the master bedroom for an intruder. Confidant she was alone, Jana made her way to the bathroom. She turned on the gold falcon water faucets, and water gushed into the circular hot tub. Then she sat on the gold toilet seat cover, looked into the wall-to-wall mirrors around her and wept.

****

The next morning, Jana bathed, dressed, changed and fed Brian Jr., worked out in her gym to Elton John's "Empty Garden," and had breakfast. After checking that Theresa and Gloria were at their posts, she walked over to her gardens to make sure the film crew wasn't destroying her flowers. To Jana's surprise, they were not yet there for the day's shoot. She decided to get more exercise until they arrived. So, she walked past the small wooden bridge over the lake and reached the woods. A cool breeze grazed her cheek and she shuddered. Suddenly, Jana felt a presence nearby. She looked around but saw no one.

Calm down. It's just your imagination, girl.

Jana ducked at a branch careening through the air.

Did somebody throw that at me? Of course it could have fallen from a tree.

Again Jana felt a menacing presence watching her. Hearing footsteps close by, Jana started to leave the woods. The footsteps grew closer. She ran, but the footsteps followed. Jana ran further then pulled open the wooden fence and entered her riding stable. Though her part-time groomsman wasn't there, she untied, then jumped onto her horse, Ginger (the name of her horse in *Sugar and Spice*). As the footsteps grew louder, Jana pressed her feet into Ginger's sides and guided her by the reins. Though Ginger was an old horse, her trotting morphed into a gallop and ended with a race past the cherry and peach trees. As Jana's strawberry-blonde locks flew in the cool morning air, Jana guided Ginger through the woods for she couldn't tell how long. Then Jana retied the horse in the stable, gave her a treat, and petted her smooth hair.

After she walked back to the gardens, Jana was happy to see the crew setting up for the day's shoot, leaving her gardens untouched. She waved to the technicians then headed back to the house.

By the time Jana entered her mansion, it was a hubbub of activity. As in the days prior, the great room was flooded with equipment and crew members. Jana made her way unharmed to the costume rack, and thanked the wardrobe woman for her costume. Changing jeans and sweatshirts in the powder room, she was happy to be shooting outdoors on such a gorgeous sunny day.

Upon making her way through the endless maze of busy people to the makeup room upstairs, Jana plopped herself down in one of the blue wingback chairs. "I feel like I live in Washington's headquarters during the Revolutionary War."

Hylas popped a piece of a candy bar into his mouth. "There's going to be a revolution all right."

"What's wrong?"

Taking a brush from the bookcase, he brushed then

tied back her hair. "Jack saw the rushes and said they're terrific."

"That's a *problem*?"

"Close your eyes." Hylas applied a rosy base to her face. "*But* he said I need to lighten Tom's makeup."

"Hylas, speaking of Tom, I walked by yesterday and overheard you telling him not to hurt me. What was *that* all about?"

Laughing as he rubbed rouge into her cheeks, Hylas said, "Girl, you have some good hearing."

"I developed that in my *School Spy* movie."

They shared a laugh.

"That's exactly what you are, honey. A little spy." He worked on her eyes, eyebrows, and eyelashes.

"Hylas, I don't mean to pry—"

"Yes, you do." He popped a piece of gum into his mouth.

"I know about the problems with Tom and his wife."

"Goody for you."

"But what does that have to do with me?"

"It doesn't."

"Hylas, please tell me what's going on."

After a long breath, he said, "Honey, there are things you don't know about. All I can tell you is…please be careful." Hylas looked at her, and complimented his work. "Beautiful."

Jana rose from the chair. "Hylas, do you think Tom will hurt me?"

His smile vanished. "I hope not, sugar. I sure hope not."

Since Jack came into the makeup room to talk to Hylas, Jana descended the stairs. Her heart sank at the middle step in recollection of finding the Jana Lane porcelain doll. After rushing down the rest of the stairs, Jana entered the great room and found Simon and Myrna having breakfast at the bar.

"Baby doll!"

"Bubala!"

They threw their respectively skinny and chubby arms around her.

Dressed in a mauve jumpsuit, Simon pressed his French rose scarf to his mouth. "I was so worried about you."

"Are you all right, bubala?" Myrna asked, stuffing a cheese pastry into her mouth then rubbing the sugar from her hands onto the sequins around her sweatshirt and sweatpants.

Jana replied, "I'm fine. Just a bit shaken."

Adjusting her tortoise shell glasses, Myrna said, "Jason told me what happened. And on a movie set!"

Simon held onto Jana like a raft in the rapids. "Who would do such a thing? I made ten percent of each doll we sold back then."

Myrna pulled at her girdle. "After hearing about this, my stomach is in total knots." She reached for another pastry.

"And what does that note mean?" asked Simon.

Jana replied through gritted teeth, "Rivera thinks it's a practical joke by someone on the crew."

"Some sick joke," said Simon.

Jana swallowed hard. "I think it was a warning for me to cancel the AIDS fundraiser at the Vanderbilt."

"Don't do it, bubala!" Myrna scouted the bar for her next pastry.

"Or to stop asking questions about what happened

to Ryan O'Halloran," Jana added.

Simon held Jana even closer. "Don't do it, baby girl. Remember your *Girl Detective* movie. Keep up the investigation until you solve the crime."

"That is exactly what I intend to do."

Jana left Simon and Myrna fretting and eating.

When she arrived at her gardens, Jana was pleasantly surprised to see her flowers still alive. However, the lawn around them was dug up with patches of grass surrounding lighting, sound, and camera equipment.

Technicians wearing muddy work boots hurried around the space, readying for the first scene of the day.

Dressed in his usual black sweatshirt and black pants, Jack motioned for Jana to join him inside a makeshift tent nearby.

"Lieutenant Rivera talked to me about the doll," Jack said rubbing his weather-worn face. "Nobody on the crew will own up to it."

"I don't believe any of them did it."

He nodded. "Be careful on set today. I asked two techs to keep an eye on you."

"Thank you, Jack."

"Let's get to work."

The first scene was a simple one, where Trevor finds Jana working in her garden and tries to insinuate himself further into her life.

As Jana and Trevor took their opening marks and waited for Jack to call for quiet, Trevor said with a tight jaw, "Jana, that police lieutenant talked to me at my hotel last night. Did you tell him I wrote you a threatening note?"

Taking a step backward, Jana used her acting skills

to reply nonchalantly, "*Did* you?"

"What do you think I *am*, some kind of psycho?"

If the straight jacket fits. "We should focus on our scene, Trevor."

He came so close their noses nearly touched. "Why do you hate me?"

"I don't hate anybody."

"That's right. You're Jana Lane. The girl who is everybody's best friend." He grimaced. "Except mine."

Jana's face softened. "Trevor, Gloria asked me to give you another chance. I told her I would."

He adjusted his leather jacket. "Take care of yourself, Jana."

"What does *that* mean?"

His dark eyes glistened like granite in the sun. "Given everything that's been going on lately, you could get hurt."

"A man is dead. I'm simply trying to find out what…or who killed him."

The prop person handed Jana a pair of gardening sheers. Jana bent down at an azalea bush, and Jack called for quiet, slate, and action.

Jana and Trevor played the scene well in each take with understandable tension between them.

After the last take, Trevor said to her, "Since you are 'giving me a second chance,' how about we eat lunch together?"

"Sorry, I have an appointment," Jana replied before he stomped off.

As the crew changed camera, lighting, and sound positions and equipment for the next scene, Jana handed the prop person the sheers then followed a costume crew member into a makeshift changing tent nearby. She quickly changed into a purple pants suit with a braided gold necklace and matching earrings.

Once back on the outdoor set, Hylas touched up Jana's makeup, and she scanned her script for a quick line refresher.

When she returned to the garden area, Jana found Tom Strong standing next to a patch of yellow tulips. With his rugged Midwestern good looks, physique, and flannel shirt and jeans, he looked like an actor on a Western film.

Jana noticed his sallow complexion and the dark circles under his eyes. Since they were preparing to shoot Tom's death scene, she assumed Hylas had worked his makeup magic. "Looks like Hylas let you have it," she said.

Digging his boots into the grass, Tom said, "I can't wait to wash this stuff off."

She smiled at the heavy makeup job. "By now you must be accustomed to makeup on film sets."

He waved his hands. Jana noticed they were heavily made up as well. "I'll never get used to it, Jana. It's just not my style."

"You'd be wearing even more makeup in the theatre."

"Thankfully, I'm not in a play."

They shared a laugh.

Scanning the area for the young actor, Tom asked, "How'd things go with Trevor this morning?"

After a sigh, Jana said, "We got through the scene."

"Rivera questioned him at the hotel last night."

"So I heard."

"He questioned me, too."

"I assumed he would."

Tom hunched his broad shoulders. "Jana, whatever you think about me, please know I would *never* hurt you...or anyone." He smiled and his lipstick cracked. "Except maybe Trevor Masquer."

She squeezed Tom's arm.

Did he just flinch? Taking advantage of the break while Jack conferred with the cinematographer about the shot, Jana asked, "Tom, is everything all right back home?"

A sad look overtook his dark eyes. "No." He forced a smile.

"Does it have something to do with Ryan O'Halloran?"

His shoulders sagged. "As Hylas keeps telling me, it's important to focus on the here and now. Maybe we *both* should give it a try."

As if on cue, the boom mike, camera, and light poles were in place, and Jack called for first positions. Tom got down with his back resting on the grass. Jana moved a few steps back.

After slate and action, Jana discovered Tom dead in the garden, checked for breathing, and screamed for help. At first tears didn't come. However, once Jana thought about finding Brian near dead two years ago, and more recently the reverend's threats and the doll with the note, tears flowed freely down her cheeks. Since a persistent airplane flew overhead ruining their audio, Jana had to repeat the scene five times. In each take, she was equally shaken and hysterical over the death of her husband.

When Jack called for lunch, Jana helped Tom off the ground.

Is he wincing in pain?

Getting to his feet, Tom said, "Thanks, Jana. Let me know if I can return the favor."

"Actually, you can."

As Jana and Tom walked back to the house, he said, "Name it."

She placed her arm through his. "I'm hosting a little event at the Vanderbilt mansion, a historic home in town. It's a fundraiser for research and treatment for AIDS. I've invited a number of celebrities and politicians, but none of them will come. Will you attend?"

"Thank you for the invitation, but I'm all booked up."

"But I didn't tell you the date."

"I'm sorry, Jana. I can't."

She unclasped their arms. "I'm guessing an AIDS fundraiser would tarnish your macho image."

Tom stopped and looked her deep in the eyes. "Jana, I've worked for many years to get to this point in my career. It's my whole life. I can't let anything take that away." He walked on to the house ahead of her.

When she arrived at the house, Jana walked past the tent set up on her front lawn for cast and crew members to eat just as Cornelius Chamberlain drove on his motorcycle past the front gate and up the long driveway. Jana and Simon Huckby met him at the front door.

At nearly seven feet tall and rail thin, the senior citizen jumped off his motorcycle, wearing beige parachute pants, a russet shirt, a thin burgundy tie, and lime suspenders. He took Jana in his long, lanky arms. "How's shooting going?"

"It's going." Her head barely cleared his waist.

Simon adjusted his rose-colored scarf then tucked it into his mauve jumpsuit. "No hug for your boyfriend?"

The cello player replied, "No hug for you, Simon. *You* get *this*." Cornelius bent down and planted a big kiss on Simon's lips.

Simon blushed. "Please, Cornelius. Not in front of the child."

Jana laughed. "You two have seen Brian and me kiss enough times." *Brian, remember him?*

Putting her arm around each of them, Jana led them inside the house. "Let's talk about the fundraiser over lunch."

Once they were seated in the sun porch with Simon and Cornelius on the white wicker glider and Jana on a white wicker rocking chair opposite them, they dug into their cob salads.

Picking a dropped corn kernel off his suspenders and popping it into his mouth, Cornelius said, "The orchestra is all set. I hired local professionals."

Jana took a sip of iced tea. "The caterer, also a local professional, is onboard, as are the staff members at the Vanderbilt."

"The invitations are all out." Simon rested his plate on a white wicker and glass end table. "I wish I had better news to report about attendance."

Jana dropped her plastic fork onto her plastic plate. "Attendance is low?"

Simon exhaled like a manic depressive. "The Vanderbilt supporters and your hippie dippy church people are coming. But no *movie people*."

"I've been trying," said Jana. "Just ask Tom

Strong."

Rubbing his receded hairline, Cornelius asked, "What are people in show business so afraid of?"

"Gay people," replied Simon with a sneer.

"But show business has *always* been populated with gay people," said Cornelius.

Simon answered, "Of course, but even though everyone in the business knew who was gay and who wasn't, our private lives remained hidden to the outside world."

"Until AIDS," said Jana.

Simon put his finger on his nose as if Jana had answered a question in a party game. "Gay people suddenly had personal lives, and they weren't very pretty."

Trying to understand, Cornelius said, "Do celebrities fear guilt by association?"

"I admit it. I'm a guilty celebrity by association." Jason stuck his flawless head into the room. "Tell me, what am I guilty *of?*"

Being the most gorgeous man in the world. "Are you still coming to our fundraiser at the local Vanderbilt mansion this Saturday night?"

"If I say yes, can I sit in here and have lunch with you instead of eating with the sweaty technicians in that big tent outside?"

Jana smiled. "Deal."

"Deal." Jason sat in the white wicker rocking chair next to Jana.

Simon and Cornelius slapped hands.

Cornelius said happily, "Our first celebrity!"

Simon stuck his tiny elbow into Cornelius' large rib. "Our *second* celebrity. Don't forget my Jana Lane."

Jason squeezed Jana closer to him. "We could never forget Jana Lane."

He smells like fresh air and citrus. I'm glad there are two other people in the room.

After taking a bite of his turkey sandwich with lettuce on whole wheat bread, Jason said, "Won't Tom Strong come? And don't a bunch of celebrities live nearby in Millbrook?"

"They all declined," said Jana, bringing her libido back in check.

"Why?"

"It's a fundraiser for AIDS," she explained.

"So?"

Simon chewed his salad like it was thorns. "Reverend *Charlatan* and his witch-burners will no doubt be protesting outside the mansion."

Clad in a skintight baby-blue ribbed shirt and black slacks, Jason shrugged his strong shoulders. "Who cares?"

Simon explained, "Plenty of people, especially celebrities who don't want their images turned to soot."

Jason unleashed his perfect smile. "I'm a coal miner's kid. I have no problem with soot."

Slapping Jason's knee playfully, Jana said, "And the local press will be there."

"Can't we use them to promote the film?" Jason asked, sipping a protein shake.

Simon put his plate on the end table. "The film's P.R. rep has a lengthy publicity tour set up for you two after the film is edited and ready for distribution." He dug into the pumpkin pouch around his waist and pulled out a large color brochure. "However, she gave Myrna and me a press piece announcing the film."

Jana scanned the brochure chronicling the film's storyline, screenwriter, and director, and each star's picture and biography. "Jason, I thought you were from Kentucky?"

"I am," he said between sandwich bites.

"This brochure says you were born and raised in Cleveland, Ohio."

Flicking back his rich blond hair, Jason laughed. "That's Myrna. She said Ohio is more *middle America* than Kentucky."

Simon threw his small hands up in the air. "See? Show business is all about...*show*. Everyone puts up a façade to appeal to the masses."

"Jason, will Myrna allow you to attend the fundraiser?" asked Cornelius with a nervous glance.

"Myrna's coming herself," said Simon.

Raising his hand as if on the witness stand, he said, "I, Jason Apollo, swear I will attend the fundraiser on Saturday night, but—"

"Here it comes," Simon moaned.

"—I'll only come if Jana Lane is my date." Jason put his arm around Jana. "What do you say, benefit organizer?"

I say I'm glad the Vanderbilt's upstairs bedrooms are off limit for the fundraiser. "Since Brian is away, I'll be honored to have you as my date, Jason."

Simon and Cornelius cheered.

"It will be great publicity for the film, and attract a lot more people to attend," said Simon.

Not to mention cause my husband to ask a lot of questions.

After she finished her lunch, Jana hurried up the spiral staircase to check on Brian Jr. When she entered his room, she found Brian Jr. asleep, and Gloria and Trevor in a heated embrace.

"What is going on in here?" Jana asked with her hand on her hip.

Breaking out of Trevor's hold, Gloria replied, "Jana, Trevor just—"

"I could see what Trevor was just doing." Jana stood by the door and pointed to the hallway. "Trevor, please leave."

Trevor's leather jacket brushed against Jana's arm. "I hope you learn your lesson soon, Jana."

"What lesson is that?" she asked with her temper rising as high as the pitch of her voice.

He smirked. "If you keep pushing me away, one day soon, I'll push back."

Once they were alone, Jana shut the door and said softly, "Gloria, I told you I don't want Trevor Masquer, or anyone from the cast or crew, in this room. Do you understand?"

Gloria fidgeted with the belt loops on her jeans. "I know, Jana. I'm sorry. We were talking downstairs and I heard Brian Jr. crying. I came up to change him, and Trevor followed me. After Brian Jr. fell asleep, we started talking." Her cheeks turned the color of her rose silk blouse. "Before I knew it, I was in his arms."

Jana let out a long breath. "Gloria, I understand you are an adult and have every right to a personal life. I also can see you like Trevor, and in his way, he likes you, too. But if I catch you with him anywhere on the second floor of this house again, I will be forced to terminate your employment here. Do you understand that?"

Gloria looked down at the carpet and nodded.

"Good. And by the way, I gave Trevor a second chance as you asked, and it didn't go too well. Now, I have a film to shoot."

Jana hurried down the stairs and walked back to the gardens, hoping the exercise would calm her down. When she arrived at the set, she changed into a black dress and black shawl then made her way to the narrow bridge over the lake to join Jason for the next scene.

"You all right?" Jason asked, looking amazing in a pin-striped gray suit.

"I'm preparing for the scene," Jana replied. *What's a little white lie between friends?*

After a light and sound test, Jack called for quiet, slate, and action.

Jana and Jason went through the scene, where the detective consoles the widow after her husband's death. The scene was so realistic the male crew members had tears in their eyes, and the females—and a couple of the men—fell in love with Jason.

When Jack had enough takes in the can, he called for a wrap.

Instead of walking back to the house, Jana headed in the opposite direction toward the riding stable. Jason followed.

"Where are you going?" he called out.

"My groomsman isn't coming in today. I want to check on my horse."

"Can I come?"

"Sure."

They walked along the outskirts of the woods until Jason said, "Great scene."

She looked away. "I'm afraid I'm not that good of an actress."

"Something wrong?"

They stopped at the wooden fence.

Jana said, "Trevor Masquer drives me crazy."

He winked. "*I* was trying to do that."

She looked into his welcoming face and smiled. "I'm glad you're here, Jason." Then she opened the fence door, and headed inside the stable. When she reached the spot where she had left her horse, Jana looked down at the ground and screamed. Ginger lay motionless at her feet.

Jason was at her side in a flash. "What happened?"

She cried, "It's Ginger!"

"What's this?" Jason picked up a note partially hidden under Ginger's head.

Jana grabbed the note. With tears clouding her eyes, she read, "When you stop, I'll stop."

Chapter 8

An hour later, the film crew had left, and attendants from the local animal hospital had taken away Ginger. Jana, Jason, and Lieutenant Rivera stood in the stable area as the sun lowered in the sky, changing the green lawn to a blanket of maize.

Scratching his raven locks, Lieutenant Rivera turned a patch of grass to winter white. "Mrs. Otley, you mentioned your horse was quite old. Couldn't she have died from old age?"

"Just before writing this note?" Jason waved the paper like a flag at a fourth of July parade.

Taking the note and sealing it in a plastic pouch, Rivera said, "We'll check this for fingerprints, but I doubt we will find any." He added with a smirk, "Except for yours and Mrs. Otley's."

Jana picked up a handful of leaves. "Somebody fed Ginger peach leaves."

"Are they toxic to horses?" Jason asked, coming to her side.

Jana nodded with tears filling her eyes. "I learned that in *Little Girl on the Ranch*."

Coming to her other side, Rivera asked, "Couldn't Ginger have eaten the leaves herself?"

Jana shook her head from side to side, and the sun turned her hair to gold. "The peach tree is far away from here. Ginger was tied up."

Rivera bent down to examine the leaves, careful not to wrinkle his dark suit. "The horse will be examined to determine the cause of death." He rose and squinted toward the sun. "Mrs. Otley, is there anyone who you think might want to hurt you?"

Rising to meet his narrow gaze, Jana replied, "As I have told you, Trevor Masquer has been belligerent to me on the set. Tom Strong seems not to trust me for some reason. Early this morning when I went out walking, I can't be sure but I think someone might have thrown a branch at me."

"I spoke with both Mr. Masquer and Mr. Strong at their hotel. They didn't appear to harbor a grudge against you, Mrs. Otley. As a matter of fact, Trevor Masquer told me *you* have been cold to *him*."

Pardon me for not enjoying being threatened.

Rivera added, "Besides, I assume rivalry among actors on a film set is common practice in Hollywood."

"It isn't." Jason's muscular back expanded. "Don't forget that Reverend Charlton and his bigoted sheep who have vowed to stop the movie...and the AIDS fundraiser at the Vanderbilt mansion."

Rivera's jaw tightened. "Let's not attack people for their religious beliefs, Mr. Apollo."

"Their *religious beliefs* don't give them the right to threaten people they don't like, lieutenant. This isn't the Spanish Inquisition."

Rivera offered Jason a pious smile. "We aren't in Hollywood, Mr. Apollo. Reverend Charlton is a valued member of this community."

Who I assume shares some of his tax-exempt donations with your office's holiday drive. "Lieutenant, are you a member of Reverend Charlton's church?"

Rivera turned away from the sun, and from Jana. "I've attended the Only Way to Heaven Church on occasion."

Jason's eyes widened. "That explains a lot."

"Are you casting stones at me based on my religion, Mr. Apollo? I believe that is discrimination."

"I'm not the one casting stones of discrimination."

Thinking about the baby born in a stable who brought peace and love, Jana raised her hands. "I think we're through here. Lieutenant, please let me know the results of the testing."

Rivera nodded. "I will also ask one of my staff to keep a watch on your property. And I will continue speaking to members of your company, and talk to your groomsman."

After not touching her dinner that evening, Jana went up the spiral stairs and heard Gloria's voice coming from Gloria's bedroom. Once she finished checking on Brian Jr., Jana stood at Gloria's doorway.

"Trevor, I can't do that!" Gloria turned to Jana then said into the phone, "Jana's here. I'll call you later."

After Gloria hung up the princess phone, Jana asked, "Can I talk to you?"

"Of course."

Gloria sat on the peach-colored chaise, and Jana joined her.

"Gloria, I appreciate how well you've been taking care of Brian Jr."

"I've grown really attached to the little guy."

"Good. Now what can't you do?"

Gloria crinkled her button nose. "Huh?"

"On the phone with Trevor. You said you *can't do* something."

Tears filled Gloria's large blue eyes. "Talk to my mother."

Thinking of it as rehearsal for when her children become teenagers, Jana asked, "Why can't you talk to your mother?"

Gloria wiped her eyes with the sleeve of her pink blouse. "Because of what Reverend Charlton did."

Jana handed Gloria a tissue from the night table. "What did Reverend Charlton do?"

After blowing her nose, Gloria answered, "I was watching his cable television show here in my bedroom. His sermon was about how some people disappoint God with their immorality."

No surprise there.

"He talked about your movie...and your fundraising benefit at the Vanderbilt."

Also no surprise there.

Gloria's face turned pale. "But then he talked about *me!*"

"*You?*"

She nodded. "He said a fine young woman in our own hometown was taken in by you and your movie production company." She added between sobs, "And I had...*relations* with a technician on the film before God punished Ryan...by killing him."

Jana looked like a pressure-cooker ready to explode. "That's outrageous!" She grabbed the phone. "I'm calling my lawyer."

Taking the phone from Jana's hand, Gloria said, "Please, don't Jana."

"Why not?"

Gloria looked down at the peach marble floor. "I told Reverend Charlton those things."

"I don't understand."

After accepting another tissue from Jana and wiping her eyes, Gloria said, "I felt so guilty about what happened with...Ryan. I couldn't tell my mother or any of my friends."

The hate light bulb went off over Jana's head. "So you told your minister."

Gloria walked to the balcony with Jana following her. The mountains looked like cutouts over the red, gold, and purple skyline. "Reverend Charlton was in the study watching the filming. We went out into the hall. He listened to me, prayed with me, and told me God would forgive my sin."

"Then he told your story on cable television." *Not to mention he blamed the film company and me for all of it.*

Crying into Jana's chest, Gloria said, "I told Trevor about the cable TV show and he became enraged. He threatened to put Reverend Charlton in his place. He also said I should talk to my mother. You offered to call a lawyer. All those things will only make it worse. This is a small town, Jana, and people can be unforgiving. I just want to crawl up in a hole and die!"

Jana stroked Gloria's back. "I've lived in this town for many years. The people I know who live here are caring, good people. The minister at the church I attend preaches about God's love and forgiveness for *everyone*." She lifted Gloria's trembling chin. "I can't believe I'm saying this, but Trevor is right. You need to talk to your mother, Gloria. Tonight. I'll watch Brian Jr. You're her daughter. She loves you. She'll understand."

"That's what Trevor said."

At least we agree on something.

Gloria gave Jana a hug. "Thank you, Jana."

As Gloria headed out of the bedroom like a court marshaled soldier, Jana said, "And stop going to Reverend Charlton's church."

Gloria nodded and was gone.

After Jana changed into her emerald silk nightgown and gold slippers, she checked in on Brian Jr. then lay on her red satin canopy bedcover and looked up at the stars through the skylights. She phoned Devon and Ed who were in the joyous throes of outdoor sports, campfires, adventures in the woods, food fights, and camp practical jokes.

Next, she called Brian. After shedding more tears for Ginger, and catching Brian up on the rest of her day, Jana said, "Poor, Ginger. She was such a good horse."

"We'll get another horse," Brian replied in a soothing tone.

Jana said like Vivian Leigh at the decaying Tara, "I don't care how many threatening notes I get, I won't stop asking questions about Ryan O'Halloran's death."

"I don't like what's going on. I want you to be careful, Jan."

"I will," replied Jana. She added with a shaky voice, "When are you coming home?"

He sighed. "A week. Maybe two."

"I wish you were here."

"How would Jason Apollo feel about that?"

"Jason has been really supportive through everything."

"I hope not *too* supportive."

"Brian, Jason Apollo may cause every other woman's heart to flutter, but my heart beats only for you." *I hope.*

"That's my girl."

Brian filled Jana in on his day then said, "I'm exhausted, babe. We'll talk again soon. Watch over Brian Jr, and yourself."

"I will."

"Have fun being Jana Lane."

Jana hung up the phone, rested her head against the satin pillow and drifted off to sleep.

****

Jana Lane ran through the woods with her heart pounding in her throat. Footsteps followed close behind her. Gasping for air, she ducked inside a bush, and held her breath. The footsteps grew louder. Jana's body shook as her assailant hovered over her then reached inside the bush to...

Jana woke with a scream and went into her bathroom to wipe the sweat off her face with a towel. After checking on Brian Jr., she settled back into bed, where she lay awake until the sun filled the room with the hope of a brighter day.

****

Jana got out of bed the next morning to the sound of Brian Jr. calling "Ma-ma" from his bedroom. Assuming Gloria was still asleep after a long night with her mother, Jana changed and fed Brian Jr., smothered him with kisses then put him back in his playpen— delighted by a new clown doll.

After showering and putting on an indigo blouse, beige slacks, and white sandals, Jana sat at her pink crushed velvet-trimmed vanity and phoned Lieutenant Rivera.

"As I expected, we found no fingerprints on the note, except yours and Jason Apollo's."

"And the cause of Ginger's death?" she asked, her heart pounding like a bass drum.

"You should work for a forensics lab, Mrs. Otley. Initial testing shows your horse appears to have died from ingesting peach leaves, which are toxic to horses." The sound of his sneer came through the phone. "I'm surprised you have a peach tree on your property, Mrs. Otley."

"As I've explained, the tree is not next to the stables."

With the noise from his creaking chair and chewed breakfast, Jana could barely hear him. "Any new developments from your home movie set?"

Jana grasped her tortoise shell hairbrush as if it were his neck. "Your minister hurt my son's nanny deeply with his on-air stone-throwing at her...and at me."

"We all have the right to our religious beliefs."

"That's what they said in Salem."

"This isn't Salem."

"Not yet." Moving to her next suspect, Jana said, "Trevor Masquer continues to behave oddly."

"I'll speak with him again." He ended the call with artificial concern. "Please let me know if there is anything else I can do to help."

How about resigning and letting a real detective have your job?

Jana hung up and phoned Brian. When she received no answer, she tried Jason at the guest cottage.

"Hi, beautiful. How are you holding up?"

Brushing her hair until her scalp burned, Jana replied, "I'm in a holding pattern."

After she filled Jason in on her phone conversation

with Lieutenant Rivera, Jason said, "I'm so sorry about Ginger. And I must admit I'm impressed with your forensic capabilities."

"You sound like Rivera."

"Ouch. I hope not." There was a pause, and then, "Religious leaders are supposed to *help* people, not use their power and wealth to try to take away people's rights and self-worth."

"You're preaching to the choir, Jason." She put down the brush and tied her hair back with an indigo and gold clasp. "Are you still up for being my date at the benefit Saturday night?"

"Rivera would have to lock me in jail to keep me away."

She laughed. "Let's hope that doesn't happen. See you later."

Jana went downstairs. Dodging various crew members in the great room, Jana made her way to the bar and served herself a bowl of oatmeal and fruit then poured a glass of orange juice.

Simon and Myrna raced toward her like pets welcoming their owner home after a long vacation.

If the tight hug didn't cause Jana to blank out, she thought Myrna's perfume would do the trick. "We heard about your murdered horse, bubala. Thank goodness you're all right. You have to finish my film!"

Wrenching her face into his tiny chest, Simon said, "Mama's here to protect you, baby doll. They can hurt your doll and your horse, but they'll never hurt *my* client!"

Jana thanked them for their concern then escaped to the kitchen, where she found Gloria and Trevor standing at one of the islands.

Walking over to them and putting her breakfast on the marble countertop, Jana asked Gloria, "Is Brian Jr. all right?"

Gloria nodded, and Jana noticed dark circles under the girl's eyes. "I came down to get him some milk."

Jana took the milk from the industrial-size refrigerator then warmed it on the oven, Jana asked, "How did things go with your mother last night?"

"Good thing I'm living here."

"What do you mean?"

"My mother said if I was still living with her, she'd throw me out."

Jana affectionately moved a loose strand of hair off Gloria's forehead. "She'll get over it, honey."

Tears brimmed in Gloria's bloodshot eyes. "She said she'll never be able to face the people in that church again."

Sounds like a plan.

The zipper of Trevor's leather jacket scraped against the countertop. "If I see that so-called reverend, he'll be meeting his maker sooner than he thought."

Jana moved him away from the island. "Calm down, Trevor."

With rage filling his round face, Trevor replied, "Why should I? That tax-exempt snake oil salesman and his hateful followers can all go to Hell, and they probably *will*."

Understanding why a woman joined the Supreme Court the year before, Jana said, "Reacting to hate with hate only breeds more hate."

Trevor shrugged off her hand. "He should pay for what he did to Gloria, and for what he's trying to do to you."

Smiling, Jana said, "Thank you for your concern, Trevor, but I'm fine."

Trevor stuck out his chest. "I'll look out for you and Gloria."

Jana stifled a giggle. "That won't be necessary, Trevor."

His face turned to stone. "Are you mocking me?"

Going back to her milk, Jana replied, "I appreciate your offer, but I can take care of myself, Trevor."

He followed her. "Like you took care of your doll and your horse?"

Gloria was at his heels like a cat with a new toy. "Leave her alone, Trevor."

His deep set eyes darkened. "No, I want to know why she hates me!"

"She doesn't hate you, Trevor."

"I made an offer to look after her, and she shunned me. Why?" His wide nose was inches away from Jana's face. "Why don't you trust me?"

Jana placed the milk on the countertop. "I don't like your temper, Trevor, or your cocky attitude."

Pushing away Gloria's hand, he said, "My first scene today takes place in your woodshed. The prop crew lined the shed walls with your pictures. It's the scene where I talk to the pictures and tell them how much I care about you, and I ask the pictures why after all I've done for you, I get so little attention from you in return. Sounds just about right, doesn't it?"

Jana met his gaze. "Then why don't you *go* there?"

Trevor pointed a thick finger at her face. "You'll never learn."

He brushed past Gloria and stormed out of the kitchen with Gloria chasing after him like a puppy playing fetch.

Jana tested the temperature of the milk, turned off the oven then took the milk and a jar of baby food up the back stairs. After feeding Brian Jr., she brought the empty containers back to the kitchen then sat on one of the swivel chairs in the breakfast nook to finish her breakfast.

Theresa arrived. After cleaning up the breakfast things in the kitchen, the maid turned on the television set. "Today's the day Savannah comes back from the dead and introduces her three husbands to one another."

Not interested in Theresa's soap opera storylines, Jana brought Devon and Ed's laundry up to their bedrooms. As she lay Devon's laundry in his bureau drawers, she heard a noise coming from the bathroom between the boys' bedrooms.

Opening the bathroom door, she found Tom Strong, vomiting over the toilet bowl. The large, tall man looked like a giant kneeling on the boys' bathroom floor. He looked up at her with embarrassment radiating from his masculine face. After flushing the toilet, he said, "I'm sorry."

Jana smiled. "No apology necessary. This bathroom and I have seen plenty of stomach aches. Do you think it's a bug, or something you ate?"

Rising slowly, he stood over the sink and braced himself against it. "I'm not sure. Hylas was doing my makeup, and I started to feel nauseous." He smiled. "He told me I'm lovesick for him."

In mommy-mode, she felt his forehead. It was warm. "Lie down on Devon's bed." She opened a cabinet next to the sink and handed him a bottle. "First take some of this. It's cherry-flavored, but it works."

"Thanks."

"When I was a child in Hollywood, I shot many scenes while under the weather or with an upset stomach. My agent, Simon, always said, 'A star is more powerful than a bug. And you are the brightest star in the heavens.'"

"I'll try to remember that," he replied with a shallow breath.

Jana took a washcloth from the closet and rested it on the sink counter. Moving the soap dish closer to him, she said, "You can wash up, too, if you like."

"Thanks again."

Without looking in the mirror, Tom routinely turned on the faucet and washed his hands and face. Jana stood motionless in shock. Realizing what had happened, Tom covered the reddish black marks on his face with the washcloth. "I burned my face at the hotel." He let out a nervous laugh. "I was trying to blow dry my hair, and the darn thing slipped. It left a mark."

Jana said calmly, "Tom, I've been doing fundraising for AIDS, and I've talked to a number of doctors."

He pushed his hands into his jeans' pockets. "It's not what you think, Jana. It was a freak accident. I'm sure it looks a lot worse than it is."

"Tom, how long have you had karposi sarcoma?"

"I don't—"

She put a hand on his quivering back. "Tom, it's okay. I understand."

Moving away like her hands were on fire, Tom said with a harrowing look on his handsome face, "You better not tell anyway, Jana. I mean it. If you do, you'll be sorry!"

She tried to calm him down. "Tom, there's no reason to be afraid."

He laughed until tears streamed down his face. "How about these reasons? The loss of my career, my dignity, and my life?"

Taking his hand, she noticed the dark mark on it. "Tom, please sit down with me."

They sat together on the edge of the bathtub. He wiped his face with the washcloth. "I'm really scared, Jana."

"I know." She held his hand. "It's a terrifying disease made more frightening by people's ignorance and prejudice."

"Like that so-called *reverend* who visited the set. Didn't Jesus heal the lepers and defend the downtrodden?"

Jana slapped her forehead. "Now I know why you don't want to attend the benefit."

He nodded. "How did you get involved in doing it?"

"Someone I worked with in Hollywood years ago recently succumbed to AIDS. I vowed to do all I could to help others, so they don't meet the same fate."

He shivered. "But everyone who has it does."

She squeezed his hand. "Tom, raising money isn't much, but it's what I can do to help. Right now it seems like our best weapon against this plague." She turned to face him. "Look at all of the diseases medical science has cured, or at least kept under control. I believe a cure will come, but we need to hire researchers and scientists, which costs money. And we need to show compassion for the victims, and take care of them as best we can."

Tears filled his dark eyes again. "I was so afraid you might catch it. That's why I kissed you so quickly in our scene."

"Tom, AIDS isn't spread by casual contact. I wish you would have told me. I could have calmed your fears."

"Hylas said I could trust you. I didn't believe him." He offered a weak smile. "But he was right. Jana Lane is pretty terrific."

It dawned on her. "*That's* what you and Hylas were talking about when I overheard you in the makeup room. And that's the reason Hylas covered your hands and face with so much makeup!"

He smiled. "Hylas has been a real friend through all this. I started feeling sick at my last film shoot. He suspected the worst and sent me to his doctor who made the diagnosis and swore secrecy. Hylas told me he would look out for me and get me through this shoot, and he has. Nobody else knows. Not even Myrna."

"And your wife?"

He laughed ironically. "I forgot about her. She knows, too. We have an…arrangement. I support her— financially. She does whatever she likes in exchange for pretending to be my wife and providing me with a…"

"Beard?"

He nodded. "She did just that…until recently."

"When you and she argued over the phone?"

He exhaled deeply. "My wife was dating another man."

"I'm sorry."

Tom shrugged his broad, sagging shoulders. "I didn't care about that. She'd done it many times before."

"Then what was the problem?"

"The problem was she let down her guard and told the guy about my…condition."

Thinking positively, Jana said, "Why would he tell anyone?"

He laughed bitterly. "For money."

"Who is paying him?"

"Me. He was blackmailing me for my paycheck on this film." Tom put his face in his hands. "Hylas told me I was a fool to pay him, but I did it anyway." He added with a closed throat. "Hylas was right. The guy asked for more money."

"Did you give it to him?"

"I didn't have to. The guy was Ryan O'Halloran."

Chapter 9

During the next two days, Jana shot her scenes, checked in on the phone with the three men in her life, looked after Brian Jr., kept Trevor's and Tom's secrets, and kept a watchful eye on everyone and everything around her.

On Friday afternoon, Jana was not needed on the set. Since it was the day before the benefit, she hopped into her station wagon and drove into town to buy a new gown, purse, and heels.

After an exhausting four hours visiting six different stores, Jana was about to give up when she found the perfect outfit and accessories—for over two hundred dollars. Vowing to sell them after the event and donate the money to the AIDS benefit, Jana paid the salivating saleswoman calculating her commission.

As Jana carefully placed her new purchases into the trunk of her car like a leprechaun storing his stack of gold, she smelled a strong combination of lilac perfume and hairspray. Jana turned to find a middle-aged woman standing next to her wearing a form-fitting, low-cut white ruffled, chiffon and taffeta dress. The woman had enough makeup on her face to shoot a silent movie, and her gigantic blonde wig scooped down over her like a ride at a theme park. A manicured, long blood-red nail touched Jana's arm. "You're Jana Lane, aren't you?"

Jana closed and locked the trunk. "Yes?"

The woman smiled and the makeup on her face cracked. "I'm Brenda Sue Charlton. Maybe you've seen me on my husband's cable television show, *The Right Reverend Rodney Show?*" Brenda Sue struggled to balance the five boxes of new outfits she had purchased for herself.

I remember you asking for money for God. I guess God is a woman size eight.

Weighted down with the packages, Brenda asked, "Would you join me for coffee?"

"Thank you, but I'm really very busy."

"It won't take long. I'd like to talk to you about Ryan O'Halloran's death."

In that case... "I guess I can spare a little time."

A few minutes later, Jana and Brenda Sue were seated in a private booth at the local diner. Brenda Sue ordered a whiskey sour and Jana asked for a cup of tea.

"Don't tell my husband, I'm having a drink," Brenda Sue said replenishing her lipstick. "I told him I quit."

"No problem," Jana replied.

Adjusting her solid gold necklace and bracelet, Brenda Sue said, "After shopping all day, I need a little something to calm my nerves." She giggled then opened her purse to retrieve a pill.

The waitress arrived with their orders. Brenda Sue took her glass from the woman's hand, popped the pill into her mouth, and swallowed the drink. Then she returned the lipstick-smeared glass to the waitress. "Give me a refill will you, honey? And my stomach is growling to beat the band. I'll have one of those shrimp cocktail thingies, too." She turned to Jana, "As the

Bible says, 'Eat and drink in abundance.'"

It does? I remember quotes about women being stoned for wearing jewelry and makeup, wearing clothes made of more than one fabric, and eating shellfish.

Looking down at her tea, Jana asked, "Mrs. Charlton, you said you would like to speak with me about Ryan O'Halloran?"

"Please call me Brenda Sue, everyone does." Puffing up her bouffant wig, Brenda Sue said in a hushed voice, "Last week when I was out shopping for new clothes, I guess I had one too many packages because I dropped all of them smack in the middle of the street." She laughed in recollection. "Mr. O'Halloran from your film crew was out shopping for cables or batteries or some doohicky for your movie, and he was sweet enough to help me load my boxes and bags into my luxury car."

More money for God I guess.

Brenda Sue fidgeted with the gold rings around her fingers. "I was feeling dizzy from not eating all day. The reverend and I live in a big estate in Millbrook. I didn't think I could make it home without fainting or something, so Mr. O'Halloran was sweet enough to offer to accompany me to lunch at that new Italian place up the street."

The waitress brought Brenda Sue her drink and shrimp cocktail. Again, Brenda Sue guzzled the drink with another pill. Dipping a shrimp into the red sauce, she said, "Over lunch, Mr. O'Halloran told me about your movie. At first, I was hesitant to listen since my husband said the film's themes are immoral and not biblical." She stuffed another shrimp into her mouth.

"But the more Mr. O'Halloran talked about the film, the more interesting it sounded." She motioned for the waitress to bring her another drink. "Jana...may I call you Jana?"

"Of course."

"I feel as if I know you."

Jana blushed. "I'm told that a lot."

"Oh, I don't mean because of your movies as a girl. I never much liked those."

Thanks.

"I mean because my husband often talks about you on his cable television show. About your homosexual agenda with your benefit."

Jana rose from her seat. "If your intention is to spew your husband's hatred and intolerance—"

Brenda Sue waved her to sit back down. "Relax, honey, before I met my husband I was a chorus girl on Broadway. I knew *lots* of gay fellas. They were the sweetest people. They took care of me when my appendix burst, and I was out of the show for two weeks. I even married one of them, but it didn't last long...for obvious reasons." She dipped and swallowed another shrimp.

"That's how I met Rodney. He and his followers were protesting outside my theatre. The show was a throwback to the days of vaudeville, so there were some numbers with chorus girls in pasties and feathers. When I came out of the stage door, Rodney told me I was a sinner. I wanted to slap his face. He explained my lifestyle was repugnant to God, and if I prayed, the Lord would forgive me. I didn't believe what he was saying, but he was so cute and determined. Besides, I was getting too old to be a chorus girl, and I knew leading roles would not be coming my way. So I got down on my knees right there in Times Square and gave my soul to the Lord.

"Afterwards, Rodney took me out to dinner then to his hotel room, and as they say, the rest is missionary history." Brenda Sue laughed at her own joke then accepted her next drink and swallowed another pill. "When I told Ryan…Mr. O'Halloran I was once in show business, he told me part of his job as Assistant Director on your film was to find new talent for the movie. And to my surprise, he said he had a role for *me* in your picture if I was…open to a new experience. I explained as a minister's wife I couldn't do anything immoral…in the film, and he said the part he had in mind for me was befitting a woman of the Lord." She ate her last shrimp.

"Jana, I'll be honest, I love my husband and his ministry. And I absolutely adore the good, kind Christian soldiers of the One Way to Heaven church. But my goal has always been to become an actress. So I was *thrilled* when Ryan…Mr. O'Halloran offered me the role in your movie."

Just as on her cable television show, black mascara suddenly streamed down Brenda Sue's cheeks as she wept. "But then that poor, sweet man went on to meet his maker in that accident during the film's shooting. So I was unable to contact him about the film role." She wiped her cheeks with her napkin. "After praying for his dear departed soul, I forgot all about acting in the movie—until I saw you this afternoon." She took Jana's hand. "Jana, the Lord brought us together today. God told me I should be in your movie, and since the Lord had to take Ryan O'Halloran to glory, *you* are the person to arrange it."

Like a woman being asked her phone number by a frisky bartender, Jana sipped her tea then replied, "Mrs. Charlton...Brenda Sue, assistant directors don't cast films during production. Casting is done by the casting director, director, and producers *before* the film begins shooting."

Brenda Sue's face dropped to her empty glass. "Are you saying there's no role for me in your film, honey?"

"That's exactly what I'm saying."

Brenda Sue's voice rose. "But he promised me! I risked everything. Do you know what would happen if the members of our church knew that I—" She stopped herself, and signaled the waitress for another drink. Then Brenda Sue said softly, "Jana, I hope you understand what I'm about to tell you." She looked from side to side. "And I hope you will keep this just between us girls."

Jana nodded.

She whispered, "Ryan O'Halloran invited me to his hotel room to...cement the deal."

"Did he offer you a contract?"

"We sealed the deal in...another manner...a *personal* manner if you will."

Ryan O'Halloran strikes again. "Brenda Sue, I am terribly sorry about what Ryan O'Halloran did to you. Unfortunately, you aren't his only victim. But please believe me, the film is cast, and there are no roles unfilled."

More mascara rivers ran down Brenda Sue's cheeks as she swallowed another drink and pill. "I'm such a stupid woman. God will punish me for this."

"Brenda Sue, at my church we look to the books of the Bible in historical context for inspiration and spirituality, not for condemnation and punishment."

Blowing her nose with her napkin, Brenda Sue said, "Tell that to my husband."

"I've tried, but he's adamant about fire and brimstone against anyone he doesn't like."

"Tell me about it." Brenda Sue sniffed.

Jana slid to the edge of her seat. "Brenda Sue, does your husband know about your...visit to Ryan O'Halloran's hotel room?"

Brenda Sue nodded and the waterworks continued. "We had a huge row about it. He told me he'd throw me out if it wasn't for how it would look to the congregation."

"When did you tell your husband about this?"

Brenda Sue blew her nose with her napkin. "We had a big argument about me being in the film. Rodney forbade it. I became enraged." She drank the last drop of her drink. "I suppose I had a bit too much to drink, and I blurted out about Ryan's hotel room by accident."

"When was this?"

"The night before Ryan died."

After consoling Brenda Sue and again swearing not to tell anyone about Brenda Sue's daytime *meeting* with Ryan O'Halloran, Jana headed back to her car.

****

The next day, since Trevor talked Gloria into attending the benefit with him, Jana asked Theresa to babysit Brian Jr.—meaning watch Theresa's evening soap operas—while everyone in the cast and crew attended the benefit.

When Saturday evening arrived, Jana made some

last minute phone calls to check on preparations for the benefit. Then, racing from her walk-in closet to her vanity and back several times, Jana dressed in a gold lame strapless gown that came in at the waist and flared out at her calves with matching shawl, heels, purse, bracelet, necklace, and earrings. She arranged her strawberry-blonde locks in spit-curls around her face then teased the rest of her hair to create a waterfall effect down to her shoulders. Brown eyeliner and mascara, blue eye shadow, raspberry rouge, and strawberry glow lip gloss made her look and smell good enough to eat.

At seven o'clock, Jason arrived at her front door wearing a Dartmouth-green pinstriped European suit and designer black shoes. His hair was gelled back off his forehead, and the natural pink in his cheeks was on luscious display.

As they drove in Brian's red Italian sports car to the Vanderbilt estate, they talked about how well the film was coming along. Then thinking about Tom Strong, she said, "Jason, if you were gay would you try to keep it from the press?"

Jason did a double-take. "Why do you ask?"

She shrugged her creamy-white shoulders. "I was thinking about how difficult it is for someone with AIDS—"

"And thinking how much more difficult it would be if someone was a gay celebrity with AIDS?"

She nodded.

He turned the steering wheel and his biceps pressed against his suit. "When you were a child star, could you have lived up to the hype your studio put out about you?"

Laughing, Jana said, "Mother Theresa couldn't have lived up to it."

Jason's handsome face took on a pensive look. "Moviegoers want their leading men to be handsome, masculine, smart, steadfast, honest, and true heroes. But how many men can fulfill those high expectations? We're human like everyone else…with all of our imperfections."

"Looking at you, I don't see any imperfections."

His dimples appeared. "They're there. You just don't see them."

"So, is every actor in Hollywood a liar?"

"Hollywood has created a fantasy world, where its stars shine brightly in a clear blue sky. But it's all as fake as blue and white lights projected onto a scrim. You can be an honest plumber, but you can't be an honest movie star. The public won't stand for it. They want perfection, and nothing less. Unfortunately, that's the reality."

She looked ahead at the winding road. "Do you think it will ever change?"

"Hopefully one day. But for now, we're all a bunch of fibbers."

They shared a laugh.

Entering through the mammoth gates of the Vanderbilt estate, Jason drove up the long entryway past trees and statues. Jana imagined what it must have been like to live in such a place.

Jana pretended she was Louise Vanderbilt, the wife of Frederick, a member of the elite class in the late nineteenth-century's Gilded Age, who purchased the property in 1895. As they drove, she marveled at the two-hundred-and-eleven acres of property, which included the gorgeous landscapes, beautiful woodlands, and gardens with fountains. When they arrived at the center of the estate, Jana gazed at the enormous, stone-columned, fifty-four-room mansion of American Beaux-Arts design.

Jason parked the car in an area designated for the benefit's guests. Then Jana and Jason made their way to a large tent set up on a grassy knoll between forests of tall trees situated on the east bank of the Hudson River with panoramic views of the river and distant Catskill Mountains. Just to the left of the tent, the orchestra played a Mozart piece. Inside the tent toward the right, waiters in white pressed uniforms stood regally behind buffet tables laden with extravagant, mouth-watering drinks, appetizers, entrees, desserts, and piles of delicate china plates and crystal glasses in all sizes. Toward the center of the tent, numerous round tables were appointed with white tablecloths, stunning flower centerpieces, and silver serving-ware. Jana was pleased her guests were not only supporting a needy and worthwhile charity, but also receiving a wonderful evening for their two-hundred dollars per person.

After Jana checked in with the caterer and wait staff, she headed over to the orchestra at the close of their first piece.

"Cornelius, the orchestra is terrific!"

The tall, thin, older gentleman wearing a black tuxedo with purple suspenders and bowtie winked at Jana behind his cello. "And you look pretty terrific yourself." After a giggle, he added, "But not as terrific as your date."

As the orchestra began their next classical piece by Handel, Jana blew Cornelius a kiss, and welcomed friends from her neighborhood, church, local arts organizations, and the boys' school. Once her hand ached from shaking so many hands, Jana joined Jason toward the far end of the tent to socialize with their co-workers from Caeneus Films.

"Here's my bubala!"

"Here's my baby doll!"

In a sequined tangerine kimono and scarlet jumpsuit respectively, Myrna and Simon rushed at Jason and Jana like flag-twirlers at half-time.

Clasping her arm through his, Myrna said, "Doesn't my Jason look handsome?"

No argument here.

"I bought him this suit when he had no clothes on."

Jana pondered that scenario.

"Except the rags from Ohio," Myrna said, causing Jason to blush.

Myrna's still touting the P.R. line about Jason coming from Ohio. Jason was right about the movie business being fakery.

"I also hired the best personal fitness trainer in LA, and look at the results!" Myrna motioned for Jason to flex his bicep.

Simon felt Jason's muscle and drooled. "That *is* impressive." Noticing Cornelius' questioning look, Simon switched gears. Not wanting to be left out of the agent hall of fame, Simon wrapped his arm around Jana's waist. "Just like when I discovered my baby doll in that play in New York City. She's still the most beautiful little girl in the world."

Like two children with bragging parents, Jana and Jason thanked Myrna and Simon then moved on to welcome Trevor and Gloria as they arrived.

Looking beautiful in a lemon gown she borrowed from Jana, Gloria clutched onto Trevor like a shield.

The girl brought out Jana's maternal instinct. "I'm glad you're feeling better, Gloria."

Gloria replied with a forced smile, "Trevor said I should forget about Reverend Charlton and move on with my life."

Standing out in a black leather suit, Trevor stared at Jana. "What do you think, Jana? Did I give Gloria good advice?"

Jana replied, "Yes, I'm glad you came."

Trevor moved in closer to Jana. "Are you glad *I'm* here, too?"

Jason moved between them. "Jana said she's pleased you both attended."

"I don't know if I believe her," Trevor replied with a cocky smirk.

A line formed on Jason's smooth forehead. "Jana doesn't lie."

Trevor laughed. "Oh, that's right. Jana Lane *never* lies. Didn't we all learn that as little children?"

"I know *I* did. And as an *adult*, I've been fortunate enough to find out first-hand it's true." Tom Strong arrived wearing a handsome three-piece gray suit.

Trevor walked over to him. "You still have your makeup on from the shoot, Tom."

Decked out in a leopard caftan, Hylas patted Tom's stooping shoulder. "I asked Tom to be my guinea pig for a new base I'm trying out. How do you think this gorgeous straight Midwestern hunk of movie star man looks?"

Before Trevor could reply, Jana said, "Hylas, I think you should ask our director." Staring down

Trevor, she added, "Trevor, have *you* seen Jack?"

With his deep-set eyes nearly disappearing inside his head, Trevor replied, "No. Why would *I* have seen him?" Trevor pouted. "Come on, Gloria, let's get something to drink."

Once Trevor and Gloria had gone, Jana said, "Thank you both for coming."

Looking down at the grass under his black boots, Tom said, "It's the least I can do."

Hylas said, "I wouldn't have missed this for a date with Cary Grant. Hm, maybe I can get Tom drunk and have my way with him?"

Jana laughed. "Enjoy, gentlemen."

As they walked away, Tom stumbled, and Hylas held onto his elbow for support. Once Tom regained his balance, they continued on to the bar area.

The film's director appeared next to Jana and Jason, wearing black pants, black turtleneck, and black blazer. Looking around the tent, he mumbled, "Big shindig. I'm hungry...so."

Jana said to his back, "Thank you for coming, Jack."

Circulating from person to person, Jana welcomed more guests and thanked them for their generosity. While they responded pleasantly, every straight woman and gay man's eyes were on Jason Apollo and Tom Strong, Hollywood's matinee idols.

Once everyone was seated at the round tables, the orchestra ended their classical piece, and Jana took the microphone positioned nearby.

"I would like to thank you all for attending this fundraiser for research and treatment for people afflicted with Acquired Immune Deficiency Syndrome.

Your generosity is so very much appreciated and needed. I have always prided myself on the fact that I live with caring and compassionate neighbors who truly value the concept of loving your neighbor as yourself. As you know, we are fortunate enough tonight to have included among our guest list, movie stars from Hollywood."

Everyone clapped for Jason and Tom who waved to the guests.

"But tonight, we are *all* stars, shining in the galaxy of hope for a brighter tomorrow for people with AIDS. Thank you again for coming. And enjoy your dinner and the music of our wonderful orchestra headed by our neighbor from Rhinebeck, Cornelius Chamberlain."

Cornelius waved his hand in the air and the orchestra switched from classical music to jazz during the appetizer course then to Broadway show tunes for the entrée course, beginning with "Camelot," offering the vision of a better world.

As the guests continued to eat their dinners, Cornelius gave his players another signal, and they switched to contemporary music.

After Jana had circulated to the last table, Jason tapped her porcelain-like shoulder. "I left Myrna and Simon at our table—recalling for the zillionth time how they discovered us. I haven't seen much of you all evening."

Jana's face turned pink. "I'm sorry, Jason. I've been busy playing host and talking to local newspaper reporters."

He unleashed a devilish grin. "Know how you can make it up to me?"

"How?"

"Dance with me."

Jason led Jana to the dance section of the tent just as the orchestra began to play "Why is it Fools Fall in Love." Resting in Jason's arms, Jana took in his fresh woodsy scent, warm blue eyes, strong jaw, and powerful physique. As his thick hand surrounded her, she said, "Thank you for coming, Jason."

"I wouldn't have missed it for the world." He held her tighter.

Feeling tired from her hosting duties, Jana rested her head on his strong shoulder.

He squeezed her closer to him.

"You've been such a good friend to me, Jason. You're so easy to talk to."

His eyes twinkled. "It's easy for me to talk to you, because I care about you."

Their gazes met.

To Jana's dismay, Chad Channing stood next to them with his cable television camera, lights, and microphone crew. After his equipment was set up and ready, Chad adjusted his gray sideburns, black toupee, and light blue leisure suit then smiled into the camera. "Hello, Hudson Valley viewers. This is Chad Channing live at Jana Lane's fundraiser for AIDS outside the Vanderbilt mansion." Coming close enough to singe Jana's eyebrows with his alcohol-scented breath, Chad said, "Jana, is the fundraiser a success?"

Jana stopped dancing with Jason. "It's a complete success, Chad. It's been a delightful evening. We raised a great deal of money from our very generous neighbors for an extremely worthy cause."

Winking into the camera, Chad adjusted the gold chain around his neck. "Jana, I notice you are here tonight with the co-star of your new comeback film, which is shooting right here in Hyde Park. Are the rumors true that you are playing Venus to Jason's Apollo on set *and* off while your hubby is out of town on business?" He let out a nasal laugh at his own joke.

Jana took a step back from Jason. "My co-stars on the film are extremely talented professionals. We are very pleased with the film so far. I believe the end result will be something to make us all proud. I hope your viewers will go see it."

Turning to Jason, Chad said, "Jason Apollo, you are truly America's heartthrob." He snorted out another laugh. "For women, that is. You could have any woman in the world. How is it you landed here in our hometown with our little Jana Lane?"

Jason turned toward the camera and lit up the cable television screen. "I consider myself quite fortunate to be sharing the screen with such a legend, and such a fine actress. I'm sure Jana Lane's fans won't be disappointed by her terrific performance in this film. I hope my fans come see it, too."

Chad pouted like a child being told to eat his green beans. "And how will your fans react to the news of your coupling with a *married* woman?"

Jason scowled. "Excuse us, our dinners are getting cold. And so are you." He led Jana back to their table.

"Adultery! Promiscuity! Immorality!"

Every head turned to the sight of Reverend Chalrton standing near the orchestra with his church's portable sound system. Dressed in his black minister's outfit, the reverend had fire and brimstone on his lips and dollar signs in his eyes. "This woman's movie, life, and so called fundraiser must be stopped! And how can decent people stop it? By turning your back right now on Jana Lane's deviant lifestyle, and supporting the Only Way to Heaven Church!"

Reverend Charlton's followers, including the Blanleys, marched behind their prophet waving signs reading, "Go To Hell, Jana Lane," "Fade Out Jana Lane's Movie," "Start a Pillar of Salt-Free Diet," "God Hates Gays," "God is Our Only Obsession," and "Amen to AIDS."

As the guests at the benefit looked on in shock and horror, the reverend and his sheep flailed their signs and chanted, "No film, no fags!" over and over, growing louder and more frenzied with each refrain.

Sitting at their table, Jason had rage in his eyes. Tyler clenched his fists. Not wanting violence, Jana held their arms.

The right reverend pointed a chubby finger at Gloria as he continued his holy war. "That young woman, as many of you know, is a member of my church. She came to me in tears and told me about the immoral practices going on inside Jana Lane's home during the making of that so-called movie. The title tells it all—*His Obsession*! Gloria Covetry was seduced then discarded by a member of the film crew. I was on the set myself, and I threatened the man with rape charges by my legal team. In response, he told me sordid information about others on the film set that would make your hair stand on end!"

Gloria wept into Trevor's chest.

Reverend Charlton stretched his hand behind a nearby tree and pushed Brenda Sue out from behind it. Mascara ran down Brenda Sue's overly made-up cheeks as Charlton said, "My own sweet, adoring wife was a victim of that film set, too. Tell them, darling." He pushed Brenda Sue forward and handed her the microphone.

Wearing all white and weeping uncontrollably, Brenda Sue looked at her husband then at Jana. After receiving a threatening glance from her husband, Brenda Sue said in a monotone voice as if reading a script, "A member of the film crew tried to lure me into his clutches. These Hollywood vultures attempted to talk me into joining the cast of their immoral film. But God gave me the power to rebuke Satan and escape their evil clutches."

I can see why she never made it in acting.

Not able to continue the charade, Brenda Sue raced off into the woods, where a hanging branch caught onto her huge wig.

Reverend Charlton picked up the microphone from the ground. "As you can see, my wonderful wife is distraught from this horrifying experience. But like little David fighting powerful Goliath, she stands strong against the decadence and perversion from Hollywood that has infiltrated our wholesome village."

Chad Channing placed his microphone at Jana's lips. "Jana, what is your reaction to the decent, God-fearing people who are begging you to stop your immoral projects and return to the traditional family values that helped build this community and this country?"

Wishing the park wasn't public property and she could throw them out, Jana took in the harrowing scene and tried to figure out what to do. Before Jana could respond, the members of her church rose and formed a line between Reverend Charlton and his followers and the benefit guests. They clasped then raised their hands high in the air. Accompanied by the orchestra, they sang "Amazing Grace" with all their might, drowning out the hate rhetoric behind them.

Tears filled Jana's eyes as she and her guests witnessed the true power of love.

Chad motioned his camera crew to follow him behind the guests' barricade to hear the other side of the story for "balance." Once at Chad's microphone, Reverend Charlton said, "Good people at home, you are witnessing a clear example of the Hollywood elite spreading their liberal might to silence the voices of the moral majority. Discriminating against the religious beliefs of the One Way to Heaven Church, these wealthy and powerful activists won't stop until atheism, promiscuity, and homosexuality are the law of the land. And how can we stop this war on everything holy? How can you protect your home and your children from Satan's clutches? By sending a tax deductable donation to God." After the reverend offered the viewers his post office box number, Chad Channing, Chad's crew, and Reverend Charlton's followers packed up and left.

Once the commotion ended, Jana's guests returned to their tables for dessert and to discuss the mind-blowing experience. Jana embraced her church members and thanked them for their support. The minister of her church, Reverend Heather, replied, "It's what Jesus would have done."

After eyeing the delectable treats on the food table, Reverend Charlton puffed out his pudgy cheeks like a hungry fish then approached Jana's table. "You may have won the battle, Mrs. Otley, but decent people will win the war against your assault on this Christian nation."

Shielding Jana, Simon replied á la Glinda in *The Wizard of Oz*, "Be gone, you have no power here."

With Tom noticeably absent from the table, Hylas smirked. "Reverend, didn't I read somewhere that your brother is gay?"

Reverend Charlton's face turned the color of their cherry jubilee. Jason rose to confront him, but Jana held him down in his seat. Once the reverend regained his composure, Jana rose and met the good reverend eye to eye. "Reverend Charlton, you can make any speeches you like, call me any name you wish, but hear this and hear it well. You will *not* stop the production of this film, you will *never* stifle my support of my gay and lesbian friends and co-workers, and my fundraising activities for AIDS will continue."

"We will see about that, Mrs. Otley." He added like an assault with a weapon, "The power of the *Lord* is on my side."

Not flinching, she replied, "And the power of *love* is on *mine*."

Looking as if he would explode, Reverend Charlton packed up his sound equipment and headed away from the tent.

As the benefit ended, Jana again thanked her guests for their support and generosity as they made their ways to their cars.

When only Jason and Jana remained, he put his arm around her and said, "You did a great job."

"Not according to Reverend Charlton and his followers."

"He'll get *his* someday soon."

Jana squeezed his hand. "Thank you for standing

by me tonight. I couldn't have done it without you."

"Yes, you could." His straight white teeth made an appearance. "But it was a lot more fun being by your side." He took her in his arms. "It felt so good, and so right."

He leaned down to kiss her, and Jana pulled away. "Jason…"

"I know. I know." Like a hormonal teenager going to take a cold shower, Jason said, "I'll get the car."

She smiled. "I'll make sure everything is in place for the cleaning crew, and meet you at the parking area shortly."

After Jana made her way through the tent and greeted the arriving cleaning crew, she took her shawl and purse from her table and walked toward the parking area. The sun had set, flooding the sky with ribbons of orange, pink, and purple, and turning the mountains and river into charcoal.

Suddenly, a gold reflection caught her eye. Jana remembered her *Jungle Girl* film, where she found the mayor in the jungle by following the reflection of his gold watch. She headed into the wooded area to see if someone might have dropped a piece of jewelry. Following the reflection, she screamed in horror at the sight of Reverend Charlton laying on the ground with blood dripping from his bald head, next to one of his own signs reading, "God's Wrath Will Be Taken."

Chapter 10

Jana hurried to the Security station at the Vanderbilt park, where a security guard phoned for an ambulance then called the police. Since most of the guests hadn't left yet, they gathered at the Security station and asked what was wrong.

Ten minutes later, once Rivera joined them at Security, Jana told Rivera, Jason, and the benefit guests everything she knew about Reverend Charlton's demise.

After the drive home, with Jason back in the guest cottage, and Gloria's bedroom door closed, Jana washed off her makeup, checked in on Brian Jr. then phoned his father.

"I want you to drop out of the movie."

"I'm not doing that, Brian."

"How can I protect you all the way from Texas?" Brian said, exhaustion, concern, and irritation flooding his voice.

Jana sat at her vanity and took off her jewelry. "I don't need you to protect me."

"Then who's going to do it, Jason Apollo?"

"I can take care of myself, Brian."

"Obviously not so far." He exhaled into the receiver. "Jan, two people and a horse have died since you began this movie. You received two threatening notes. Throw everybody the hell out of our house and get back to being a wife and mother."

Jana rubbed her sore feet. "I *am* a wife and mother, Brian. And I am *also* finishing this film." Moving on to massaging her temples, she said, "I think someone in the company is a murderer, and I intend to find out who it is."

"Why can't you leave it to Rivera?"

She brushed her hair. "Rivera seems incapable. I think I can do this, Brian."

"Babe, this isn't a Jana Lane movie where you save little Timmy from the bad pirates. This is real life. You could get killed!"

"I don't think so."

"What do you mean?"

Jana took off her gown and slipped into her lime satin nightgown. "Think about it, Brian. Whoever murdered Ryan O'Halloran, Ginger, and Reverend Charlton could have murdered me, too. But he didn't. Instead he sent me threatening notes. Why?"

"To try to get you to stay out of it, which you should!"

Pulling down the ruby-red satin bed cover, she said, "Right, except for the 'you should' part. But why hasn't he killed me, too?"

"Dumb luck on your part?"

"Wrong. He wants to keep me alive...to finish the picture."

"Are you sure that's the reason?"

"What else can it be? As long as this film is still in production, I'm safe. There was a similar story in my *School Spy* film, where the school principal didn't murder me because he needed me to win the spelling bee. I know it's an odd analogy, but the reasoning makes sense."

Breathing out deeply, Brian said, "I hope you're right, babe."

"I *know* I'm right." She stretched out on the king size bed. "Two people and an animal have died. I won't crawl up in a hole and let the murderer go free because of two threatening notes."

"What if Charlton's followers make him a martyr and come after you?"

"They're sheep not wolves."

"I don't like it, Jan."

"Then come home."

"Babe, I love you…and I miss you. But I can't. Not yet."

"All right. Then you can be my Hastings over the telephone."

He laughed. "Who knew I married Hercule Poirot?"

"Please, Brian?"

He sighed. "Okay, Hercule, tell me about each of your suspects, and what you have on them."

"Do I have your promise of strict confidentiality regarding what I am about to share with you?"

"Who am I going to tell in Texas?"

Jana sat up in bed with her knees folded in the yoga position. "Trevor Masquer was quite miffed when Ryan O'Halloran critiqued Trevor's acting on set and intimated he would tell everyone Trevor was cast in the film due to nepotism by his father, the director. Trevor was also quite angry, as we all were, at Reverend Charlton's threats against us tonight at the benefit. Trevor constantly tries to ingratiate himself to me, and when I back off, he becomes enraged."

"Enraged at Jana Lane, how is that possible?"

"Stick to the investigation, Hastings."

They shared a laugh.

Brian asked, "Could your director be the murderer…trying to protect his son?"

"Jack Capello seems to care more about the film than his son." She thought a moment. "However, he *was* angry by Ryan's attempted takeover of the director's duties. And Trevor mentioned Ryan had an affair with Jack's ex-wife."

"Being a jealous husband doesn't necessarily make him a murderer. Just ask me. Next suspect?"

"Tom Strong was being blackmailed by Ryan O'Halloran who was sleeping with Tom's wife."

"Why was Tom paying to keep his wife's affair a secret? I sure wouldn't."

"Very funny. Tom is in the closet—as a gay man." *And as a person with AIDS.*

"And Ryan knew it?"

"Bingo."

"Yikes! The behind the scenes movie is more dramatic than the film itself."

Jana lay on her stomach with her legs bent at the knees, her ankles crossed—a famous Jana Lane pose. "Hylas, our makeup and hair person on the film seems to be unrequitedly devoted to Tom."

"Meaning Hylas might have committed the crimes to protect Tom Strong?"

"Hey, you're good at this."

"And I wasn't even in your girl detective movie."

"I'm ignoring that." Jana pressed her eyes closed in an effort to think harder. "Of course Simon and Myrna Buller would do anything to protect the film." *And their commissions.* "But I can't imagine what either of them would have against Ryan O'Halloran, or anyone else on the film."

"Which brings us to Jason Apollo."

Jana's heart skipped a beat. "Jason was enraged, and rightfully so, at Reverend Charlton's verbal attacks at the benefit, but why would he kill the assistant director on the film? Besides, I've gotten to know Jason quite well, and I can't believe he would hurt anyone."

Brian cleared his throat.

"You know what I mean." Jana took in a deep breath. "And I'm sorry to say it, but there's another suspect, your son's nanny. Let's not forget Gloria was seduced by Ryan O'Halloran, and falsely promised stardom—as reported by Charlton on his cable television show. That makes her a pretty good suspect for the two murders."

"If I thought Gloria could hurt you, or anyone, I'd never have hired her and asked her to live in our home. Are we at the end of your suspect list?"

"There's one more. Reverend Charlton's wife. Ryan O'Halloran did a Gloria repeat performance with her. Brenda Sue's husband found out and hit the holy roof."

"So you think she might have knocked off both of them for revenge."

"And a nice inheritance *for God.*"

"Isn't she the woman who cries on cable television and asks for donations?"

"That's her."

"Do you think she's capable of murdering two people?"

Jana sighed. "As I learned when my character stole

a loaf of bread in *The Adorable Orphan*, anyone can be driven to do almost anything under the right circumstances."

Brian giggled. "Does that mean you might play the perky little orphan again?"

"I have to call you late at night more often. You're a barrel of laughs."

"They'll go with the barrels under my eyes. Speaking of restless nights, are you still having that dream about being chased in the woods?"

Not wanting him to worry, Jana answered, "They've become commonplace. I don't think I could sleep without them."

"Why do you think you're having those dreams, babe?"

After a pause, Jana said, "I think I'm running away from something, and searching for something at the same time. Does that make sense?"

"Sorry, babe. I dissect houses not brains, though being an architect does drive me crazy."

They shared another laugh.

"Honey, thank you for staying up to talk with me. I'm breathing normally for the first time all evening. I miss you. Come home soon."

Brian's voice was full of love and exhaustion. "As soon as I can, babe. Be careful. And take care of my two favorite people."

Hopefully that means Brian Jr. and me. After hanging up the white and gold French provincial phone, Jana lay in bed looking up at the rose and blue canopy above her.

What am I missing? There's something buried in the recesses of my mind. What is it?

Jana drifted off to sleep.

****

Jana Lane ran through the woods with her captor gaining ground behind her. A branch grazed her forehead, causing it to bleed. She twisted an ankle, but kept on running. The path narrowed. A fallen tree trunk blocked her path. She ran in terror in the opposite direction smack into the arms of...

She woke in the morning with a gasp and tried to normalize her pounding heart. After showering, changing into a malt-colored skirt and a pink angora sweater, Jana checked in on Brian Jr. Coming out of his room, she ran head first into Trevor coming from Gloria's bedroom.

"What are you doing here?" Jana asked with a no-nonsense look in her blue eyes.

Trevor tucked his shirt into his pants then put on his leather jacket. "Gloria was upset by what the so called *reverend* said about her last night. I came over to comfort her. Thanks to your *rules*, she asked me to leave."

Jana looked past him to Gloria's closed bedroom door. "From now on, comfort Gloria *downstairs* only."

His large forehead came toward Jana like a shark attack. "Why do I have the feeling you don't like me?"

She glared at him. "Probably because I don't."

Before he could respond, Jana walked past him and knocked on Gloria's door. Gloria opened it and Jana went inside, closing the door after her.

"Are you all right, Gloria?"

Tying the belt of her pink cotton robe, Gloria answered, "I'm better now."

"I'm sorry about what Reverend Charlton did to

you last night."

Gloria sat on her bed and wiped her eyes with a tissue. "I was taught not to speak ill of the dead, but I'm glad that monster is gone."

Jana patted her on the shoulder. "I checked in on Brian Jr., so take your time getting dressed."

"Thanks, Jana. You're the best."

After Jana left the room and closed the bedroom door, she heard Gloria's whimpering.

Jana called out, "Gloria, would you like to come with me to my church today?"

After a pause, Gloria replied, "I think I'd like that."

"Good. I'll wait for you."

An hour later, Jana and Gloria sat in a front pew in the small church, gazing at the historic pipe organ and gorgeous stained-glass windows depicting the life of Jesus of Nazareth. Sharing a hymnal, they sang hymns and recited prayers.

Reverend Heather's sermon was a powerful call to be Christ-like by taking care of the poor, destitute, and outcasts, and working for equality and social justice. The minister spoke of God's love for everyone, rich or poor, dark or light, gay or straight. When she talked of God's forgiveness for all, Jana noticed tears brimming in Gloria's red eyes.

Gloria took a tissue out of the sky-blue purse that matched her dress. "Jana, I've done some terrible things."

Jana placed her hand on Gloria's back. "You're forgiven, Gloria."

"But you don't know everything I've done."

To Jana's surprise, Reverend Heather ended the service with a call to pray for Reverend Charlton.

After the service ended, Jana and Gloria shook Reverend Heather's hand at the church doorway. The minister said to Gloria, "I saw you at the benefit last night. You are a brave young woman. May God's blessing be upon you."

As they walked to the station wagon, Gloria said to Jana, "Thank you for bringing me here."

Jana smiled. "I hope you'll come again."

"I'd like that, Jana."

Jana put her arm around Gloria and they left for home.

For the rest of the day, Jana played with Brian Jr. in his bedroom, ate dinner, and studied her lines in bed until she drifted off to sleep.

****

The following morning, amidst the usual film company chaos in the great room, Jana ate scrambled eggs, yogurt, and melon with a chaser of orange juice then answered the front door to Lieutenant Rivera.

Standing under the prism chandelier, Rivera scratched his raven curls and a flood of white covered the saffron marble floor around his feet. "Mrs. Otley, I have been investigating Reverend Charlton's murder."

So you finally believe there is a murderer on the loose?

"Mrs. Charlton was understandably too hysterical to be interviewed."

I'm sure.

"But I've spoken to most of the people who were at the benefit—except for your film crew. May I use one of the rooms in your house to interview members of your production company about the murder of Reverend Charlton last evening?"

"Of course. We are shooting outside today. You can use the music room."

He pulled down the jacket of his blue suit. "And you will alert everyone who was at the benefit that I will need to speak to him or her by the end of the day today?"

Jana nodded then led Rivera to the music room.

Next, she notified Jack of Rivera's plans for the day. When members of Caeneus Films were not needed on the set, they were summoned by a production assistant to the music room for interrogation by the lieutenant.

****

Lieutenant Rivera sat at Jana's Louis XIV desk opposite a Degas painting on the sky-blue wall. Pushing aside the gold pen with the musical note on it, he placed his pad and bitten down pencil on the desk.

Sitting across from the desk on a Prussian blue couch, Gloria Covetry and Trevor Masquer looked like truant children in the principal's office.

Rivera said, "Normally I would interview you each separately, but no one is being charged with anything. This is an informal interview."

"We didn't see anything," offered Gloria, pulling her daisy-colored summer dress over her knees.

Rivera scratched his thick hair and the blue desk blotter turned white. "Miss Covetry, I understand Reverend Charlton mentioned you in his speech last night at the benefit."

She bit at a nail. "He was concerned a member of his congregation was working in this house."

Rivera turned toward Gloria as if aiming a spotlight in a dark alley. "And wasn't he also concerned

Ryan O'Halloran dangled stardom in front of you in exchange for sexual intercourse, which you agreed to?"

Tears welled up in Gloria's eyes. "I made a terrible mistake."

"As Reverend Charlton pointed out on his cable television show, then again at Mrs. Otley's AIDS benefit, didn't he?"

Gloria nodded between sniffs.

"And before he passed on, did Mr. O'Halloran make good on his offer to you?"

"No," Gloria replied lowering her head.

Rivera focused on Trevor Masquer. "I understand Mr. O'Halloran criticized *your* acting on the set, Mr. Masquer."

Pulling up the collar of his leather jacket, Trevor replied as if talking to a judge in juvenile detention hall, "The so-called reverend and our ruthlessly ambitious assistant director were parasites who both deserved what they got."

Rivera looked up from his notes. "And did *you* give them what they 'deserved,' Mr. Masquer?"

"Of course not," Gloria replied rapidly. Trevor and I were together the day Ryan O'Halloran was...the day of the accident, and again at the benefit last night."

"But as I understand it, there were *many* people milling around the shooting location on the day of Mr. O'Halloran's...death. And you two were among them."

Sliding to the edge of the couch, Trevor said with a chip the size of Atlantis on his shoulder, "We didn't do it. Any other questions, lieutenant?"

Rivera replied, "As a matter of fact, yes." After Trevor groaned, Rivera asked, "Isn't it true Reverend Charlton wanted to stop film production? And isn't it also true, Mr. Masquer, this is your first film role, what some might call your *big break*?"

"Yes and yes," Trevor replied with his large brown eyes narrowing.

Rivera took in Gloria and Trevor. "Can you each tell me where you were when Reverend Charlton was hit over the head with the sign last evening?"

Gloria raised her hand as if in school. After Rivera nodded in her direction, she said, "At the completion of the benefit, I went to get my car in the parking area reserved for guests of the benefit."

"Mr. Masquer?"

"I went for a walk in the woods," said Trevor, looking bored with the discussion.

"And why is that?" Rivera asked.

"To take a leak." Scratching his wide nose, Trevor added, "I drank a lot of champagne."

"Were all the porta-potties in use?"

"I'm not an animal, lieutenant. I don't piss in a corral."

"But you...urinated in the woods?" Rivera asked.

"Nobody was around," Trevor replied.

Readying his pencil, Rivera asked, "Did you see or hear Reverend Charlton, or anyone else?"

Trevor crunched his round face. "I just said I didn't see anyone. After I did my business, I zipped up and met Gloria at the parking area."

Gloria added, "We were ready to leave when we heard Jana making a commotion with the security guard."

"At least something got Jana Lane's attention. I sure don't," said Trevor behind a sneer. "Anything else, lieutenant?"

Rivera was glad to end the interview. "I believe that's all."

****

Jana and Tom Strong stood outside the columned front door of Jana's mansion. Both dressed in business suits, they prepared to shoot a short, simple scene in the film, where Jana and her husband wish one another a good day then drive off.

Dressed in his usual all-black attire, Jack Capello rubbed at the dark bags under his eyes and called for quiet, slate, and action.

Jana turned to Tom and delivered her first line casually. She noticed a dazed look in his eyes. When Tom did not say his response line, Jana paused then offered an ad-lib in an effort to jar Tom's memory. However, he looked even more confused and disoriented.

Jack yelled, "Cut! Margie, show Tom the script."

As the script supervisor spoke with Tom, Jana could not help but notice how drawn and haggard he looked, even with Hylas' expert and abundant makeup.

After another slate, Jack called for take two. "Action!"

As if it was happening for the first time, Jana waved to her husband and said her line. Again Tom looked shaken and confused. Again she offered a cue to help him. And again Jack shouted, "Cut!" This time Jack approached Tom. "What's wrong?"

Tom replied with a weak smile, "I'm sorry, Jack. I didn't get much sleep last night...with the benefit and the murder of that wacko reverend."

Jana nodded with empathy. "Yes, Jack, we're all a bit on edge. I'm sure we'll get it right for the next take."

Scratching his calloused face, Jack said, "All right. Let's roll and slate again for take three. Action!"

This time Jana gave her line, and Tom answered with his. Jana delivered her next line, and Tom looked at her in fear. She purposely stammered then said, "Sorry, I flubbed the line."

Jack exhaled loudly. "All right, everyone. Places for take four. And *please*, let's concentrate and get this done."

During the slate, Jana whispered to Tom, "You can do this, Tom. Just repeat your two lines over and over in your head." She reminded him of his lines, and he nodded.

If Tom's acting wasn't exactly inspired, he said his lines correctly for the fourth take, and Jack yelled, "Cut! Print! Let's move on to the next location."

Back in the music room, Simon Huckby and Cornelius Chamberlain sat on the Prussian blue couch, looking like nervous relatives in a hospital waiting room.

Still sitting behind the desk, Lieutenant Rivera gazed at the bald little man in the coral jumpsuit. "Mr. Huckby, as Jana Lane's discoverer and agent, how did you feel when Reverend Charlton disparaged her chaste image and threatened to shut down production of the film?"

Fiddling with his apricot ascot, Simon replied, "It awakened my maternal instincts to protect my girl from predators."

Cornelius dug his long elbow into Simon's tiny rib. "But of course Simon would never hurt a fly."

"The reverend was a *gnat* all right," said Simon with his brown eyes raised to the blue and white crystal chandelier.

After jotting down a note, Rivera asked the tall, thin man in the leather motorcycle outfit, "Mr. Chamberlain, you and Mr. Huckby assisted Mrs. Otley in planning the AIDS Fundraising Benefit at the Vanderbilt. And at the benefit you split your time conducting the orchestra and playing the cello. Is that correct?"

Cornelius tucked his long, thin legs underneath him. "That's correct."

"And you and Mr. Huckby are...*domestic partners*. Is *that* correct?"

Cornelius beamed like a lighthouse. "It is."

"It's never too late for love," Simon added with an air kiss caught by Cornelius.

"So, Mr. Chamberlain, I imagine you were also quite upset when Reverend Charlton disparaged the film, the benefit, Mrs. Otley, and the homosexual community."

Cornelius' smile turned to a frown. "I was, but that doesn't mean—"

"Where were you at the time of the murder, Mr. Chamberlain?"

Cornelius rubbed his wet palms on his knees. "I packed up my cello then loaded it with the other musical instruments into a van in the parking area. Then I met up with Simon and my motorcycle in another area of the same parking lot."

"And you, Mr. Huckby?"

Simon answered with a sniff, "After making sure my baby doll was all right after that vicious attack by the so-called *reverend*, I walked into the woods."

Rivera's bushy eyebrows rose to his forehead.

"And why is that?"

"To get a better view of the sunset. It was beautiful. Then I met Cornelius in the parking area as he said."

"Did you see or hear anyone in the woods?"

"Only the squirrels and the birds," replied Simon.

"Then you drove home on Mr. Chamberlain's motorcycle?"

Simon replied, "We saw my baby doll with the security guard, so we offered our help." Looking down his nose at Rivera, Simon added, "*You* hadn't arrived yet."

Rivera asked, "And Mr. Huckby, you were also at the set the day Ryan O'Halloran suffered his…accident?"

"I was." Simon raised his tiny chin and pointed to the Jana Lane film posters on the wall. "I never left my baby doll alone at a shoot in the past, and I'm not starting now."

With a concerned look on his long, thin face, Cornelius asked, "Is there a problem with that, lieutenant?"

Lieutenant Rivera smiled like the cat who ate the canary. "No problem at all." Rivera asked, "Do you have AIDS?"

They replied in unison. "No."

"How do you address Reverend Charlton's charges that your agenda was violating his and his followers' religious beliefs?"

Cornelius said, "Lieutenant, though originally sanctioning same-sex marriages, the Roman Church decreed death by burning at the stake for homosexuals in 390 AD. Hence the term, 'faggot.' The members of the tax-exempt Only Way to Heaven Church can believe whatever they like, but when they lobby politically to take away our civil rights, we will fight back."

"And is that what you did?"

Cornelius and Simon stared at the Persian rug on the floor.

Finally Cornelius said, "Lieutenant Rivera, if Simon and I killed everyone who hated homosexuals, the streets would be lined with dead bodies."

Simon added, "Including yours, lieutenant."

****

Jana and Jason sat on the wooden deck behind Jana's mansion with their feet resting in the warm, bubbling water of the hot tub. Jana always had butterflies in her stomach before shooting a scene, but for this scene the butterflies had butterflies.

Jason Apollo was dressed in Yale-blue Speedos with a flesh colored g-string underneath them for his upcoming rear nude scene, which would no doubt make the film a box office bonanza. His body was oiled, giving his muscles a Greek god aura.

All of the hours in her home gym paid off royally. Jana looked gorgeous in a cerise bikini. Her body was firm and shapely. A light spray tan followed by an application of skin cream gave her skin a smooth and silky glow. Like a magic trick, Jana was costumed with a second top (with a thin flesh-colored strap in the back) hidden underneath her bikini top. She prayed there would not be a costume malfunction. Though the set was cleared of all personnel except those needed to shoot the love scene, Jana kept telling herself she was an actress, and the scene was just like any other.

Except I will be making love to the sexiest man in America.

Seeming to read her mind, Jason winked at her and whispered in her ear, "I may make a few intentional mistakes, so we can do as many takes of this scene as possible."

She hit him playfully on one of the bulging muscles in his thighs. "Let's just do this as we rehearsed it at the guest cottage."

He pressed his large shoulder against her. "We never rehearsed the last part of the scene."

After the technical aspects of the scene were ready, Jack called for quiet, slate, and action. Jana and Jason exchanged their dialogue in a casual, believable, and intimate manner, clearly two people who had gone through an ordeal together, and were very much attracted to one another. As they delivered their dialogue, the warm, massaging bubbles surrounding her feet didn't do much to relax her.

Jana and Jason repeated that part of the scene several times until Jack was satisfied all the angles had been filmed appropriately. Then they moved on to the final part of the scene.

Upon hearing Jack's call for action, Jason slipped off his Speedos, revealing his round, firm, muscular naked buttocks (except for the flesh-colored g-string straps) for the money shot. He slowly entered the hot tub and beckoned for Jana to join him. Jana slid into the steamy hot tub, and Jason took her in his muscular arms. She wrapped her hands around his v-shaped back as the bubbles massaged their bodies and drew them in closer to one another. As their lips met, Jana felt his warm breath on her skin, and his woodsy, citrus scent filled her head. His thick fingers caressed her hair, neck, and shoulders. They kissed again and his body enveloped hers. Reaching around her back, Jason unfastened the top of her outer bikini top, revealing Jana's bare back (except for the flesh-colored string) to the camera. With her chest pressed against his mountainous pectoral muscles, they kissed again, more deeply. And again. And again. "Cut!"

Though Jack had called for the scene to end, Jason continued the kiss. Not wanting it to end, but knowing it must, Jana pulled away just as the wardrobe mistress helped them out of the hot tub and wrapped a robe around each of them.

Jack almost smiled. "Good work. We got it in one take!"

As the crew packed up the equipment to move to the next shooting location, Jana stood on the deck and tied the belt of the robe around her waist. "That was unprofessional, Jason."

He shrugged. "We nailed it in one take, didn't we?"

Jana searched his handsome face. "I'm talking about *after* Jack called cut."

Taking her by the hand, Jason moved Jana to a private area of the deck. "Jana, I'm not going to pretend I don't want to be with you. I do. And I think you want to be with me, too. I've never connected with anyone like I connect with you. If this film has brought us together, so be it."

Jana felt her blood pressure rise higher than the hot tub thermostat. "I'm married, Jason."

"*Are* you?"

"What does *that* mean?"

His eyes bore into her. "It means I know what I felt when we kissed."

"I was *acting*!"

"*Were* you?"

Good question.

He held her hands next to his heart. "This film shoot will be over in one day, Jana. I'll be heading back to California, and you'll be staying here." He blinked back tears. "It tears me up inside to think about it."

"Jason, we'll remain friends. We can talk on the telephone."

"Like you talk to your husband?" He took her in his arms. "I want more than that, Jana. I want you. *All* of you. With *me*. *Always*." He kissed her passionately. "I don't want to leave here without you."

Jana came up for air. "Jason—"

He put his fingertips to her lips. "Don't listen to me, or to your husband, or even to yourself. Just listen to your heart." He walked into the house, and Jana summoned the strength to change for her next scene.

Chapter 11

Lieutenant Rivera sat behind the desk in Jana's music room interviewing Jack Capello, Myrna Buller, Tom Strong, and Hylas Summer, who were perched on the Prussian blue couch like plastic ducks at an arcade.

Rivera readied his pencil. "Can you each please tell me where you were after Reverend Charlton left the benefit?"

In pink spandex slacks and a sequined gold tube-top, Myrna replied, "I'll go first, bubala." Pushing her tortoise shell glasses up her surgically altered nose, she said, "Jack and I were walking to the parking area and I realized I forgot my handbag. So I went back to retrieve it. Then I met up with these three guys at our rented car. Of course when we saw the commotion at the security area, we went over to see what was going on."

Dressed all in black as usual, Jack rubbed his dry fingertips against his craggy cheeks. "Myrna said it right."

Rivera asked, "Mr. Summer?"

Hylas adjusted the lavender embroidered tunic over his skintight jeans. "I went to look for Tom."

"And where were you, Mr. Strong?" Rivera asked, scratching his head and unleashing a snowstorm in front of him.

With his torso hunched over his knees, the rugged-looking actor aimed his weary eyes at the lieutenant. "I was in the porta-potty."

Rivera let his eyes take in Hollywood's favorite cowboy. "Mr. Strong, are you well?"

Stifling a cough, Tom replied, "Something I ate last night must not have agreed with me."

Rivera nodded. "Mr. Summer, after finding Mr. Strong at the porta-potty, did you both walk together to the parking area?"

"No." Hylas patted Tom's knee. "Tom felt sick again...as he said...from something he ate. Before going back into the porta-potty, he asked me to go on ahead to the parking lot. He said he'd meet up with me there."

"And did he?"

Hylas replied, "Obviously. He's *here* isn't he, honey?"

Rivera said, "Mr. Summer, are you a homosexual?"

Hylas replied proudly, "I am."

"Do you have AIDS?"

"No."

The fat rolls in Myrna's arms bounced like rubber on a trampoline. "Bubala, none of my clients have AIDS."

Hylas added, "Lieutenant, despite what Reverend Charlton preached, gay and AIDS are not synonymous."

Rivera leaned over the desk and his elbows turned white. "Mr. Summer, as a homosexual, and as a crew member on the film, how did you feel when Reverend Charlton expressed his religious belief that homosexuality is a sin?"

Digging his manicured nails into the couch, Hylas

replied, "The only sin around here was Reverend Charlton's hatred and bigotry."

Myrna waved her red nails. "Lieutenant, these gentlemen, like all my clients, are menches. They kvetch from time to time, but they would never hurt a fly buzzing on their noses."

Flipping through his notes, Rivera asked, "Mr. Strong and Mr. Capello, I did some…research on your personal lives. And I heard a rumor that Ryan O'Halloran had an affair with both of your wives. Is that true?"

Jack scratched at the rope-like skin on the back of his neck. "It ended our marriage."

Rivera responded, "And yet you hired Mr. O'Halloran as your Assistant Director on this film, despite your creative and…personal differences."

"Ryan was my A.D. on a number of films. I saw no reason to change that," said Jack.

"And you, Mr. Strong?" asked Rivera.

Tom looked as if woken from a daydream. "Excuse me?"

Rivera lost his patience. "Did your wife have an affair with Ryan O'Halloran?"

"Oh." Tom added as an afterthought, "I believe so."

"And didn't that *bother* you?"

Tom's shoulders dropped. "No."

After writing a few notes, Rivera asked, "Mr. Capello, why are you hiding the fact that Trevor Masquer is your son?"

"*I'm* not the one hiding it," replied Jack.

Myrna scratched one of her necks. "Trevor doesn't want to be known as a star's kid, bubala. He wants to make it on his own."

"Yet, his first film role is directed by his father," said Rivera behind a snide grin.

Tom held his stomach. "Lieutenant, may I be excused?"

Hylas put his hand on Tom's shoulder. "Poor Tom still has food poisoning." He grimaced and rubbed his own stomach in a bad attempt at acting. "I may be coming down with it, too."

"You may go," Rivera said. "But don't go too far."

Next on the couch were Jana and Jason. Jason wore a pale blue polo shirt that accentuated each of his rippling muscles along with tight jeans. Jana was in her outfit for the upcoming scene, a coral button-down blouse and burnt sienna slacks. Her hair was blown dry and arranged stylishly around her shoulders.

Rivera said, "Can you both please go over your movements during the presumed time of Reverend Charlton's murder?"

"Even television detectives don't interview suspects in pairs and groups, lieutenant."

Rivera replied, "Mrs. Otley, I am not charging anyone. I am simply asking questions. Speaking of questions, can you please answer *mine*?"

After Jana and Jason again reviewed their whereabouts prior to the murder, Rivera threw his hands up in the air. "Ten suspects, at least, and *nobody* has an alibi."

"I don't understand, lieutenant," Jana said.

Rivera scratched madly at his dark hair, unleashing a cavalcade of white onto the desk. "During the time we think Reverend Charlton was hit with the sign, each person I interviewed today was alone." He read down his list. "Trevor Masquer was urinating in the woods."

"Why am I not surprised?" Jana said with a sigh.

Rivera continued with another scratch. "Gloria Covetry walked alone to her car, and Cornelius Chamberlain walked alone to his motorcycle. After checking on you, Mrs. Otley, Simon Huckby gazed in solitude at the sunset from the woods. Since Myrna Buller forgot her purse, and Tom Strong was ill in the porta-potty, they, along with their companions, Jack Capello and Hylas Summer, walked to the parking area alone." Rivera slid to the edge of his seat. "Which leaves the two of you, who separated when Mrs. Otley checked on the cleaning crew. Meaning, you both walked to the parking area without a chaperone."

Jason said, "So any of us could have killed Reverend Charlton."

"Precisely." Rivera closed his notepad in frustration. "And everyone had a motive, including the two of you as stars of the film Reverend Charlton and his followers were determined to stop."

Jason asked, "Why should Charlton's or anyone's religious beliefs dictate how people can or can't live their lives? There are many religions, prophets, and holy books. Not to mention numerous translations and revisions of them throughout the years. Isn't that why our forefathers created the Constitution, and its guarantee of freedom from religion?"

"And freedom *of* religion." Rivera sat back in his chair. "The question as I see it is: did someone kill because of religion?"

"It wouldn't be the first time."

Rivera asked, "Are you disparaging the concept of religion, Mrs. Otley?"

"No, Lieutenant Rivera, just the corrupt people who abuse it for their own gain."

Jason said, "Jana isn't a suspect. I can't imagine she would destroy her doll, kill her horse, and send herself threatening notes."

"Jason wouldn't do any of those things either. Certainly my agent, Simon, and his partner, Cornelius, wouldn't as well. And Myrna Buller wouldn't kill her own client, Ryan O'Halloran."

"You are both assuming we are dealing with one perpetrator. There may be more than one," Rivera said, shifting his gaze between them.

Jana said, "Lieutenant, can we focus back on Reverend Charlton's murder?"

"By all means." He motioned for her to continue.

"Were there any fingerprints found on the sign used by the murderer?"

"No," Rivera replied.

Jason asked, "And nobody saw or heard anything?"

"Not a thing." Rivera couldn't help wondering if the reverend's murder was a group effort as in the case of one of Agatha Christie's famous mysteries. He looked down at his white-covered notepad. "And many of the people I interviewed had a motive to kill Ryan O'Halloran as well."

Jana smiled. "So now you believe Ryan O'Halloran's death was not accidental?"

"I didn't say that." Rivera narrowed his eyes. "I am simply checking out *all* possibilities, Mrs. Otley. Which brings me to the two of you. Had either of you worked with Mr. O'Halloran in the past?"

Jason shrugged. "I worked with him on a few films."

"Did you two ever argue?"

Jason laughed. "Quite the opposite. We became friends."

Rivera asked, "Were you involved with the documentary Mr. O'Halloran directed?"

"No." Jason looked thoughtful. "But he interviewed my father for it."

Shifting his gaze, and his suspicions, to Jana, Rivera asked, "And how about you, Mrs. Otley?"

"I met Ryan on this film." Jana added, "Lieutenant, did you speak to Jack, Trevor, Tom, and Gloria about *their* association with Ryan O'Halloran?"

Rivera flipped through his notes. "Yes, Mrs. Otley. Based on what you told me, and what I found in my investigation, they *each* have a motive." He closed his notepad. "You are both free to go."

****

Jana went upstairs to check on Brian Jr. Stroking his pink cheek, Jana asked Gloria, "How's Brian Jr.?"

Gloria replied, "Fine. I fed him, changed his diaper, played find the teddy bear with him, read him a story, and just put him down for a nap."

Looking at Gloria's ruffled tea-rose dress, Jana asked, "How come you're dressed up?"

Gloria's face turned the color of the blouse. "Trevor is coming over tonight. I wanted to wear something special."

Jana said, "Gloria, please remember, Trevor is not permitted on this floor of the house. Is that clear?"

"Sure." Gloria covered Brian Jr. with his blanky. "The baby is so adorable. I'm really attached to him. He likes me, too."

"So I see." Jana sat on the rocking chair. "How are

things with your mother?"

Gloria seemed out of breath. "She still hasn't forgiven me for the thing with Ryan O'Halloran." Running a tense hand through her blonde hair, she added, "Trevor thinks I should move back in with my mother, take my old bedroom where she's sleeping now, and insist upon sorting this out with her. But don't worry. I'm not going anywhere, Jana. This place feels like home. I like it here." She smiled. "And I have no intentions of leaving."

Jana ate lunch at the great room bar while Simon hung over her like a vulture at a garbage dump.

"I heard your love scene with Jason Apollo was quite the scorcher. Have America's heartthrob and my baby girl discussed *future plans*?"

Crunching on a toasted walnut from her Waldorf salad, Jana said, "My future plans are with my husband and my children."

"Don't get all high and mighty with me, missy. Remember who discovered you." Simon lifted the eyeglasses on a chain around his neck and rubbed them furiously with a marigold and lust-red polka dot silk handkerchief. "Wouldn't you rather be married to someone in the business?"

She speared some greens with her fork. "I guess that's something we will never know, Simon."

Filling his plate with chicken, shrimp, salmon, duck, and assorted side dishes, Simon said, "Let's not be too hasty, baby doll. Elizabeth Taylor Warner was married seven times, twice to the same man. And he was in show business!"

"And *I* am married to Brian...once and hopefully always. And Brian is not, and never will be, in show business."

Simon sat next to her and put his tiny arm around her. The scents from the smorgasbord on his plate made Jana's head spin. "What a gorgeous couple you and Jason would make. Hollywood royalty. Think of all the good press we would get if you married Jason Apollo. You'd make the cover of every magazine in the country. It would be bigger than Princess Grace's car accident in Monaco!"

After swallowing the last bite of her salad, and washing it down with orange juice, Jana rose. "Simon, talk to Myrna. I have to prepare for my next scene."

As she walked away, Simon said to Jana's back, "If you won't marry someone in show business, how about letting me launch Devon and Ed? Kid actors are coming back."

Jana called out over her shoulder, "No, Simon."

"Brian Jr.?" he hollered.

"No!"

Ten minutes later, Jana stood in her woods surrounded by trees, lighting equipment, cameras, sound equipment, harried crew members, and Trevor Masquer. Dressed in his usual black leather jacket and black chino pants, Trevor said to Jana, "You must be happy about how the benefit ended."

She shivered. "Though I detested nearly everything the man said, I didn't wish any harm to come to Reverend Charlton."

"How can you say that after what that nutcase said about Gloria? And after what he said about *you*?"

"*My* religion teaches me if we each attack those who attack us, what we will have left is a lot of wounded people."

Trevor snapped a twig off a tree. "I'm glad he's dead. I hate evil people like that."

She winced. "'Evil people like that?' You sound a great deal like Reverend Charlton."

He grinned. "Charlton doesn't sound like much of anything anymore." He threw down the twig. "How's your investigation going, Jana?"

"You mean *Lieutenant Rivera's* investigation."

"I say what I mean. You should try it some time."

Jana rested her hand on a tall oak tree. "All right, how's this? You're my top suspect. Trevor."

Trevor pressed his black boot against a fallen branch and kicked it away. "I don't understand why you have to be such a bitch."

Jana's eyes doubled in size. "*Excuse* me?"

"Every time I try to be friendly with you, you bite off my head. I'll bet you don't talk that way to Jason Apollo."

"How I talk to Jason Apollo is none of your business, Trevor."

He shrugged his broad shoulders. "Why not? Everyone else is talking about you and Jason." He smirked at her. "I wonder how your *husband* feels about that."

Stopping herself from strangling him with a camera cable, Jana said, "I understand you have a date with Gloria tonight, Trevor. If I catch you upstairs, I'm calling Jason to throw you out."

"I'll bet you call Jason whether I go upstairs or not."

Hylas appeared and powdered Trevor's large forehead. "You two play nice now."

"Easier said than done," grumbled Jana.

"I heard that," Trevor said as he took his beginning mark for the first shot.

Jack stood over Trevor as if scolding a rambunctious child. "Are we ready, Trevor?"

Trevor replied like a spoiled brat, "*I'm* ready. Ask *her* if *she's* ready."

Taking her first position, Jana said, "Trevor, what did I tell you about speaking to your…speaking to the director in that tone?"

Jack rubbed his wrinkled forehead. "Thanks, Jana, but I've heard much worse."

"No doubt at home," she mumbled.

After Jack moved behind the camera, Trevor glared at Jana. "You're just like my mother. Always ready to put down my father and me, but falling all over the first stud who gives you a second look."

"Okay, Trevor, let's talk about your *parents*," Jana said, daring him.

"Forget it."

Simon and Myrna arrived and wished Jana and Trevor a good scene.

They grunted "thanks" in return, and the agents moved to the sidelines to watch.

Hylas freshened up Jana's makeup and hair. "Have some patience with the boy, honey. He suffers from *Me-Me-Me Syndrome*." Accomplishing his obvious goal of making Jana smile, Hylas left the shooting area.

Jack called for quiet, slate, and action. The first shot was a long shot from behind as Trevor chased Jana through the forest for rejecting him and going with the detective. Since a long wooden track had been constructed on the ground, the camera was able to move quickly, following them through the woods. After the crew solved a few technical problems, the shot was completed successfully in three takes.

As the technicians moved the camera to the opposite side, Jana stood behind a tree and took a sip of water. After she placed her water bottle back on the ground, she felt a hand on her shoulder—propelling her into the tree. Checking her shoulder, Jana was glad to see she was not hurt, and her costume was unscathed. Looking around, Jana saw no one in her immediate vicinity. She asked Jack, Hylas, Myrna, Simon, and even Trevor if any of them had seen someone push her, and they all said they had not.

Trevor stood next to her. "Maybe it's your time of month, and you got dizzy."

Before Jana could wipe the smirk off his face with a poison ivy leaf, Hylas repaired their makeup and hair then Jack called for quiet, slate, and action. They did the scene as a long shot of Trevor chasing Jana through the woods with the camera in front of them.

Next, Jana and Trevor ran the same path for the close-up shot on Trevor in all his maniacal glory. In both cases, given the technical intricacies of the shot, they nailed it in three takes.

Finally, they did the scene one last time for Jana's close-up. Thankful for her comfortable sneakers, and many hours in her home gym, Jana ran yet again through the woods, followed by Trevor. This time the light of the camera was in her eyes, and she had difficulty staying on the path. Seeing only white light in front of her, Jana felt Trevor's breath on her neck. She looked back and shrieked at his face, reminding her of a pit bull on the attack. Jana wasn't sure in which direction to run next. She remembered the advice she was given while shooting *Jungle Girl*, to look down at the ground and follow the clear path. Jana felt Trevor getting closer. Sweat streamed down her back and soaked her blouse and the seat of her pants. Her heart hammered in her chest like a drum. Growing dizzy but struggling to stay vertical, she cried out and kept running toward the blinding white light in the direction of the clear path.

Am I making the movie, or dreaming?

Her legs wobbled underneath her. Her breathing was labored. Gasping for air in near hysterical panic, just when she thought she could run no father, Jana felt two strong arms wrap around her torso, and she fell into Jason's welcoming chest.

"Cut! Good one!" Jack said. "Let's set up for the next scene. Jana you're wrapped for today. Jason and Trevor we need you for the fight scene."

Holding onto Jason with all her might, Jana looked up at his handsome face. "Thank you for catching me."

Jason squeezed her tightly and smiled. "My pleasure."

Chapter 12

That evening, Jana kissed Brian Jr. and read him a story, which he gratefully critiqued afterward, "Li-li!" So Jana did two encore performances for her appreciative audience.

After she ate a quick dinner, she phoned Devon, Ed, then Brian. Once she told Brian about her day—leaving out the film's love scene and the personal proposal by Jason—Jana sat on the rim of her circular hot tub. Surrounded by wall-to-wall mirrors, she turned on the gold falcon faucets and said into the phone, "Gloria told me you called today."

"I missed you. I'm glad Gloria's taking good care of Brian Jr., and of you. I'm not wild about that Trevor character, though."

"Join the club." Jana poured chamomile, vanilla, and juniper berries into the bath water. "When are you coming home, Brian?"

He exhaled loudly. "I hope soon, babe. Things are totally nuts here, but I'm working as hard as I can to please everyone and come home to you." After the sound of some commotion, Brian said, "I have to go, Jan. Some people are here for a meeting."

"I love you, Brian."

He whispered, "I love you even more. Take care of yourself, Brian Jr., and Gloria. I'll be home soon."

After hanging up the phone, Jana released the

tensions of the day by soaking in a hot bath. Then, she dried off with a fluffy white towel, brushed her hair, and dressed in a white pirate shirt, mahogany slacks, and white sandals.

With the sun casting a crimson glow over her property, Jana walked through her backyard past her gardens, over her bridge, and past the stables through the woods. Feeling like Little Red Riding Hood, she felt a presence nearby. Jana winced at the recollection of her dreams and that afternoon's shoot. So she walked faster, nearly breaking into a run, until she reached the guest cottage.

Jason opened the door of the guest cottage, looking amazing in a purple tank top, jeans, and sandals. He welcomed her inside onto the brown suede couch next to the brick fireplace. After serving them lemonade, Jason sat next to her.

Jana said, "I'll never get used to not shooting in sequence. It's like living life in reverse."

"We're up to it, partner."

Jana and Jason rehearsed their scene for the next morning's shoot. As two talented professionals, they hit every emotional beat in the scene, where the detective cautions the ex-child star about her new young assistant—Trevor. At the end of the scene, Jason leaned in and lightly kissed her lips.

Leaning away from him, Jana said, "There's no kiss at the end of this scene."

His eyes glistened. "I know." He went into the kitchenette for more lemonade. "You should be careful."

"Of *you*?"

"Of *Trevor*." Jason's huge biceps bulged as he

refilled their drinks.

Jana flicked back her blonde locks. "Trevor's just a spoiled brat."

Sitting back down next to her, Jason said, "Who has issues with you, and access to your house...your son...and his nanny. I'm worried about you!"

Jana slid to the edge of the couch. "Jason, we have to talk."

His dimples appeared. "Aren't we talking?"

"I mean about us."

"Is there an *us*?"

She took his thick hand in hers. "Jason, you are not like any other man I've ever met." Squeezing his hand, she said, "Most straight men I've known have a male bravado...a sullen wall that can be difficult to penetrate. You're different."

"Thanks...I think."

She laughed. "You are open and warm and sweet. I've loved getting to know you these last weeks."

"But?"

"Jason, under different circumstances, we might date and, who knows, even become a couple one day. But—"

"This isn't the day?"

"No. I am happily married."

"Are you?"

Jana stared him down. "Jason, I love my husband and my children and my life in Hyde Park. As much as I adore working with you and spending time with you, all I can offer you is my friendship. It wouldn't be fair of me to say I could give you anything else."

He turned away, unleashing his chiseled profile. "I think you're making a big mistake."

"That's exactly what I'm trying *not* to do."

"I've been with a lot of women, Jana. But it's never been like this. I understand we haven't known each other for a long time, but it's been long enough for me to know I love you, and I want to spend the rest of my life with you."

She rested her hand on his thick forearm. "And I'm incredibly flattered, Jason. But at this point in my life, I can be your colleague, friend, and co-sleuth, but nothing more. Can you accept that?"

"I guess I'll have to…for now. But be warned, I'm not giving up on the future." He rested back on the couch. "As they say, 'it's all in the timing.'"

"I'm a woman of my word, Jason." *Now I just have to take my eyes off you and follow my own dictum.*

After a long exhale, he said, "Do you want to go over the scene again?"

Back to the investigation. "Actually, I'd like to talk about the murders."

Have you made any headway, Nora?"

Her fists clenched. "It's so frustrating."

"What do you mean?"

"I can't believe I'm saying this, but Rivera is right."

"About what?"

Jana's blue eyes were clear and focused. "Not including you and me, there are eight suspects, all with motives—at least to kill Charlton, and all with opportunity to have killed Ryan O'Halloran, Reverend Charlton, and Ginger."

"What about the threats to *you*?"

She squeezed his arm. "Jason, today in the woods, before my last take, I felt someone push me."

"I didn't see anyone."

"Neither did anyone else. But I don't think I imagined it. Just like I don't think I imagined someone pushing me into my pool that day or throwing a branch at me before we found Ginger." She bit at a nail. "I believe the same person killed Ryan, Charlton, and Ginger, and he or she wants to stop me from discovering the identity of the killer."

Putting his hand on her knee, he said, "Who do you think it is?"

She rose and paced the cozy room. "That's what I've been trying to figure out over the last week. But I think I've made a huge mistake."

"Explain it to Nick."

She paused at the fireplace. "I've been having this feeling...like I'm forgetting something. And I think this is it." Jana tented her fingers. "In *The Girl Detective*, the character I played got too caught up with investigating the suspects, until her father the police chief gave her some good advice."

Jason leaned forward with his elbows on his knees, and his pectoral muscles swelled. "What was that?"

Stick to the investigation, girl. Turning back the pages of time, she answered, "He said to look into the backgrounds and secrets of the *victims*, and the killer will be revealed." Jana looked out the small window with the blue shutters. "And that's *exactly* what I'm going to do."

"Want some help?"

"Thanks, but I think I have to do this alone."

Jana wished Jason a good night and headed back to the main house. The last part of the sunset had left a gray glow over her property with just enough light to make the path visible. As Jana walked through the woods, she had a strong sensation someone was following her. After looking behind and to the sides of her and seeing no one, she continued on the path.

Don't let your imagination get the best of you. One foot in front of the other and you'll be home soon.

Jana breathed a sigh of relief as she came out of the woods and continued the rest of the way back to her mansion.

When Jana arrived home, she ran into Trevor in the front hallway. He looked up at the grandfather clock, and said, "Home late, aren't we?"

Jana sat on the window seat and motioned for Trevor to join her. "Trevor, your father knew Ryan O'Halloran pretty well, didn't he?"

Trevor sat and rested his back against a throw pillow. "Sure. They worked together on a bunch of films."

"I hope this isn't too painful for you to talk about." *But I'll ask you anyway.* "When your mother had her…friendship with O'Halloran, and it destroyed your parents' marriage, why did your father continue to work with Ryan?"

Trevor looked up at the prism chandelier hanging from the cathedral ceiling. "My father was out working all the time. My mother was crazy lonely. I tried to keep her company, but I was up to my ears at school. Ryan dazzled stars in front of her eyes, took advantage of her then dumped her. Dad wanted no part of her after that, and she wanted nothing to do with him. I think Ryan was a conduit for something that was already broken between my folks. Dad didn't blame Ryan as much as he blamed himself."

"But Ryan followed the same pattern with other women."

"So I've heard."

"And Ryan wanted to become a film director."

Trevor pulled the collar of his leather jacket over his neck. "After Ryan directed that documentary film in Kentucky, he wanted more than anything to direct a feature." He pressed his knee against hers. "To do that, Ryan needed clout...and money."

Pulling her knees up under her chin, Jana asked, "And how did Ryan go about trying to get those things?"

"You saw how Ryan tried to take over the set that day in your study, and how he asked Myrna Buller about her upcoming film packages."

"You said Ryan also needed *money*. What was he doing to get it?"

Trevor's cheeks turned pink. "Blackmailing me."

Jana's eyes doubled in size. "When? Why?"

"Ryan knew I'm Jack Capello's son, and he threatened to tell the press if I didn't grease his greedy palms."

"Which you *did*?"

"I *had* to, or everyone would think I got the role due to nepotism." He shrugged. "Luckily, Ryan's not a problem anymore." Trevor rested a hand on her knee.

Jana rose. "Thanks for the information, Trevor."

He glared at her. "That's it? You got what you wanted, and now I'm dismissed?"

Running her fingers through her hair, Jana said, "Trevor, it's been a long day."

"But we were finally becoming friends. Can't we talk a while longer?"

"Trevor, I need to check on Brian Jr."

"That's why you hired Gloria."

"He's *my* child, Trevor."

Trevor stood so close his breath caused her eyelashes to flutter. "That didn't seem to bother you when you were at the guest cottage with Jason."

"How do *you* know where I was?"

He raised his palms. "Where else would you be but with your boyfriend?"

Jana opened the front door and pushed Trevor out. "Goodnight, Trevor."

"Why do you keep shunning me, Jana? Why can't we be friends?"

"When you learn some manners, we can talk. Until then, good night."

"You'll regret—"

Jana closed the door and locked it. After mounting the spiral staircase, she heard Gloria in Brian Jr.'s room. Standing to the side of the doorway, Jana listened to Gloria talking to him in his crib.

"You're such a good boy, Brian. And I love you very much. If you don't know it now, you'll know it when you get older. When your father gets back home, I'll be leaving you for a little while. But I'll be back. And we'll be a family."

Brian Jr. cooed, "Ma-ma."

Jana entered the room. "Are you leaving us, Gloria?"

Gloria pulled at her blue polyester robe. "I'm going to straighten myself out, Jana...to be a good role model for Brian Jr., and for myself. When Brian gets home, I need to make amends with my mother then get my life together."

Straightening Brian Jr.'s blanky in his crib, Jana asked, "And how are you going to do that?"

Gloria sat on the rocking chair. "I've been watching you, Jana, and I've decided I want to be more like you."

Jana laughed. "I think one of me is more than enough."

"I mean, I want to respect myself more. Not let people push me around."

"You can start with breaking things off with Trevor."

Gloria smiled in adoration. "Trevor is so self-confidant."

He certainly thinks the world of himself.

"Trevor's a real sweety. He's really smart, too, and he works very hard."

So did Hitler.

Before drifting off to sleep, Brian Jr. concurred with, "Tre no."

"My friendship with Trevor is special to me, Jana, just like yours is with Jason Apollo."

"Gloria, you know my friendship with Jason is just that…friendship, and nothing more?"

"Whatever you say." Gloria looked down at the dancing bears on the tile floor. "Trevor is helping me not to make the same mistake again."

Jana leaned on the changing table. "You mean what happened with Ryan O'Halloran?"

Gloria nodded. "And with Rev. Charlton."

That's my sleuth cue. "Gloria, after you told Rev. Charlton about what happened with you and Ryan, did he speak to Ryan?"

Gloria nodded. "I saw them go into the hallway

together while you were shooting your scene in the study."

"Before Ryan was killed?"

Gloria nodded again, and her eyes filled with tears. "I overheard Rev. Charlton threaten Ryan, saying he would tell the press Ryan was the crew member who seduced me...if Ryan didn't give him information about other people on the set."

The old Salem Witch Trials/McCarthyism/gays in the military name names routine. "And did Ryan give Charlton any information?"

"I couldn't hear because Ryan started whispering."

I wonder if Ryan was telling Charlton about Tom Strong having AIDS?

Jana moved to the window and looked out at the blackness. "Gloria, do you know anything about Rev. Charlton's personal life?"

"I know he's been married three times, and his ministry is very popular...at the church and on cable television."

"Do you know where he went to school, or what he did before he became a minister?"

She shrugged her small shoulders. "Sorry, I don't."

"How about his wife, Brenda Sue? With Rev. Charlton passed away, his widow must be quite wealthy."

"I heard she left town with the head deacon to start a theatre company."

Jana bit her lip. "Do you know anything else about Rev. Charlton?"

She thought hard. "I remember Rev. Charlton mentioned in a sermon how the Lord delivered him from prison. At the time, I thought he meant the shackles of sin. Now I'm not so sure."

"Did he ever mention committing a crime or having a record?"

A crease formed on Gloria's forehead. "I think he talked about some problem in Arizona...before he moved to New York."

"When was that?"

As if finding a needle in a haystack, Gloria replied, "He said it was ten years ago."

"What did he do?"

Like a medium at the end of a session, Gloria rose and took Jana's hand. "Jana, I wish I could give you more information, but I've told you all I know about Rev. Charlton." Her young face hardened. "Except that I'm never going back to his church. Good night, Jana."

Gloria left the room.

****

The next day, Jana woke, showered, worked out in her home gym, fed and changed Brian Jr., ate breakfast, and shot her scene with Jason on the sun porch.

When they finished, he turned to her on the opposite side of the glider. "What are you going to do with your afternoon off?"

Ducking a moving light, Jana said, "It's back to the investigation."

"Can I help?"

Touching up Jason's makeup for the next scene, Hylas said, "Nancy Drew has to go it alone today, honey. You're in the next shot. So go and change your suit."

Myrna and Simon stood at the doorway, barely escaping a boom mike being carried to the next room. "Be careful, baby girl," shouted Simon. Pulling at the diaper underneath his magenta jumpsuit, he added, "I'm putting out feelers for your next film!"

"This movie isn't finished yet, bubalas." Myrna scratched one of the stomachs housed within her sequined goldenrod sundress. "Stay out of trouble, Jana!"

"I will." *I hope.*

Jana hurried out of the room, careful not to run into the technicians flinging around camera cables like lariats at a rodeo.

After checking in again on Brian Jr., she changed from her beige business suit and high heels into her Vassar sweatshirt, jeans, and sneakers. Then she ran down the back stairs as she pulled her hair into a ponytail.

Upon entering the kitchen, she told Theresa she would be gone for a few hours.

Sitting in front of the television set at the kitchen island in her maid's uniform, Theresa replied, "You'll miss Ebony finding out her cousin is really her mother."

"I think I'll survive," replied Jana.

"Hopefully Ebony will, too."

Jana opened the door to her four-car garage, pressed the button on the garage wall to open the garage door, slid into the driver's seat of her station wagon, and drove off.

After parking the car in a hotel lot, Jana made her way up to the third floor and knocked on the door at the end of the hallway.

"It's open."

Jana let herself inside the hotel room and sighed at the sight of Tom Strong shivering under the covers of the hotel room bed. She rested a bag on the end table then took a seat on a green wingback chair next to the king size bed. "Thank you for agreeing to see me, Tom. I brought you some lunch from the shoot. Chicken soup, chicken pot pie, garden salad, a fruit cup, and a glass of chocolate milk." The delicious scents filled the room.

Tom smiled weakly. "Thanks, Jana. I'm not hungry right now. Hylas was here early this morning with breakfast, and unfortunately, I wasn't able to keep it down."

"Perhaps later." She took his hand. It felt cold and clammy. "Have you seen a doctor, Tom?"

He shook his head no. "It's too risky."

"But you need care."

"I phoned Hylas' doctor in LA. He's mailing me some medication." He shrugged his sagging shoulders. "I doubt it will do much good."

She noticed a new lesion on his face, or perhaps it had been there all along, hidden by the makeup. "Can I get you anything, Tom?"

The skin on his face sagged. "How about a smile?"

She unleashed the famous Jana Lane smile. "We're going to find a cure for this horrible disease."

"I'll be waiting," he said followed by a cough.

"They figured out a way to transplant an artificial heart in someone. Can a cure for AIDS be far behind?"

"There's a great deal of money and public support for people with heart disease. People with AIDS don't have that luxury."

"We're going to change that, Tom."

He nodded, clearly not believing it. "Good thing I don't have any scenes today."

"Will you be well enough to shoot tomorrow?"

"I'll have to be." He looked at her through bloodshot eyes. "Luckily my scenes are almost finished."

"Don't you think you should tell Jack about your condition?"

His face was suddenly ablaze. "Absolutely not. Nobody can know about this! Do you understand, Jana? *Do you*?"

Jana replied, "Yes, Tom, of course I understand your concerns, but if Jack knows, he can make…accommodations on the set."

He flailed his arms like a modern dancer. "No! Jana, this is vitally important. No one, and I mean no one, can know about this. If anybody…if somebody leaks this to the press, I'll be ruined."

Moving the covers over his shoulders again, Jana said, "All right, Tom. I promise I won't tell anyone."

Looking as if he just ran a marathon, Tom rested his head back on the pillow propped up against the green headboard. "I have only two scenes left. I'll get through them."

"When you are wrapped, will someone be going back with you to California?"

He nodded. "Hylas hired an assistant to cover for him on the film so he can accompany me."

"Hylas has been a good friend to you."

As if just realizing it, Tom said, "I guess he has."

She squeezed his hand. "We will miss you."

He said with a dry throat, "All things come to an end, Jana."

Rising to the bureau and pouring Tom a glass of water, Jana asked, "Will you see your wife when you're back in LA?"

He laughed bitterly. "I doubt it."

She handed him the glass of water. "Tom, do you mind if I ask you a few questions about Ryan O'Halloran?"

"You're too young to be Miss Marple."

They shared a laugh.

After taking a sip of water, Tom said, "Sure, go ahead. It doesn't look like I'll be going out partying today."

She squeezed his shoulder. "You told me Ryan O'Halloran had learned about your diagnosis from your wife, and he was blackmailing you to keep it a secret."

"That's right."

Jana sat at the edge of the bed. "I've found out Ryan was also blackmailing someone else."

"I'm not surprised."

"I know Ryan wanted to be a film director, and of course it takes a great deal of money to shoot a film, but the capital is generally put up by the production company. So why did Ryan need access to so much money?"

After taking in a labored breath, Tom said, "Obviously I didn't talk to the guy much, but I remember him saying something about making a bad business deal."

"A bad investment?"

"I believe so."

"Do you remember the name of the company?"

Tom rubbed his wet forehead. "I believe it was Norotech." He smiled. "At least my memory isn't totally gone."

Sitting back down on the chair, Jana said, "Do you know when this was, or anything about the company?"

"Sorry, Jana. That's all I remember."

Jana visited with Tom a while longer. When his eyelids started to droop, reminiscent of her behavior on the set as a child star, she gave him a cherry candy and left the hotel.

Her next stop was the Hyde Park Library. Built in 1927, the stone building resembled a home more than a library. Jana parked her car on the street then walked up the front stoop to the front door with a window on each side of it. Entering the library, she passed a brick fireplace and spoke with the woman at the information desk. Since the library did not have the information Jana requested, she drove on to her alma mater.

A half hour later, Jana was seated toward the rear of the Vassar College library. Taking a cue from her *School Spy* movie, she sat in front of a microfiche machine searching through old articles from various newspapers.

Jana found a ten-year-old article from an Arizona newspaper reporting the arrest and imprisonment of used car salesman Murray Johnson, and his stripper wife, for robbing a string of jewelry stores in the city of Buckeye. Looking at the picture on the top of the article, Jana was sure the man was…

Reverend Rodney Charlton.

Searching through later articles, Jana found he'd served his time, divorced his wife, and moved out of town.

After reading more articles, Jana realized he followed the same pattern with a different wife—a cocktail waitress—in Dubuque, Iowa two years later, culminating in getting another divorce—and a mail order minister's license upon leaving prison.

At that point, he must have moved to New York and found Brenda Sue, wife number three. And as they say, the rest is history.

Jana searched through various news sources, but she was unable to find any connection between so-called Reverend Charlton and the list of suspects.

Next, Jana looked for information on Norotech. After an exhaustive search, she located a two-year-old bankruptcy notice for the Boston-based medical technology company. Scrolling through the list of investors, she found only one familiar name, Ryan O'Halloran.

Scouting through articles from Los Angeles, Jana charted Ryan's career as an assistant director of various films directed by Jack Capello for Caeneus Films. Prior to the current film, Jack and Ryan worked with Tom Strong and Jason Apollo on two other movies packaged by Myrna Buller. Hylas Summer was listed as makeup and hair supervisor for both films.

That must have been when Ryan met Tom's wife, and when Ryan got to know Jason. I wonder if Jason's mention of his childhood in Kentucky prompted Ryan to make his documentary.

Jana located then read through the publicity material for Ryan's documentary film.

Now I see why Ryan needed all that money.

Not able to get financing from a studio, Ryan had bankrolled the entire production, which though already shot had fallen short of the funds needed for editing and distribution. Jana read about the film's content, displaced coal miners in Lynch, Kentucky, and how many of them were ill and recently unemployed. In addition to photographs of the mountain range and coal mines, Jana perused photographs of the coal miners interviewed for the documentary. She stopped at the last photograph—of Frank Appleton.

What a nice-looking man. He must be Jason's father. Of course nobody would know that since Jason's press biography lists Jason as hailing from Ohio, and his last name as Apollo.

Finished with her investigation and coming up empty, Jana returned the microfiche slides to the librarian. She shuddered at the feeling she was being watched. Looking around the library, she didn't see anyone watching her.

Get it together, Jana.

Since the crew would still be filming at her house, Jana asked the librarian for one last group of microfiche slides then took them back to the machine. Curious to see what Jason looked like when Myrna discovered him playing Romeo in his high school play, Jana perused his hometown newspaper during the time he would have been a high school senior. Not able to find anything about the play or Jason, Jana was about to give up.

Come on, girl, how important is it to see Jason Appleton as an eighteen year old before his Hollywood transformation into the heartthrob Jason Apollo? Pretty important.

Finally, she located an article about the senior play at Lynch's public high school, *You Can't Take It with You.*

That's not it.

Jana continued looking until she came upon information about a private high school in Lynch and their senior play, *Romeo and Juliet.* She searched the article's picture for the student playing the leading role, and found Romeo in his tunic, tights, and cap.

Jason was a lot thinner, younger, less self-confidant looking, and he had a different nose. But I can see the resemblance.

As she read the article, Jana's eyes doubled in size.

Oh my God!

Chapter 13

Jana drove through the small town streets with questions racing through her brain. As she tried desperately to connect the dots, more questions popped up in her mind. Jana pulled into her garage and found the film crew had gone. After checking in on Brian Jr., she ran down the back stairs through the French doors and across her backyard. Desperate to talk to Jason, she ran past her garden and stable and through the woods.

Since it was twilight, the woods had an eerie glow. Jana stumbled on the dark path and hurt her ankle, but she kept going, intent on talking to Jason. Suddenly, she felt a breath on her neck.

It's probably just a breeze. Don't let your imagination play tricks on you. You have to find Jason.

Jana continued to run. Coming around a bend, she felt a hand on her back.

It must be a branch. Keep going.

Jana ran on until someone pushed her, and she fell into a tree. She looked around and saw nothing but trees matted against a purple and orange backdrop. Realizing she was in danger, but trying to remain calm, Jana used a move from *Jungle Girl*. After climbing the nearest tree, she snapped off a branch and held it in front of her as a weapon.

Her heart pounded away the seconds then minutes. Then looking around and seeing no one, Jana slowly descended the tree, holding the branch as a shield. Suddenly, a hand grasped her foot and pulled it downward. Jana screamed and landed on her stomach. After getting to her feet, she ran, hearing footsteps behind her.

Darting out of the forest, Jana dived into the lake. Recalling an underwater stroke she learned for *Young Mermaid*, Jana swam for what seemed like an eternity. When her lungs finally gave out, she came up gasping for air. Upon seeing the guest cottage in the distance, illuminated only by the moonlight, Jana called out for Jason. Hearing no response, she climbed out of the lake and ran toward the cottage.

Jana felt a hand grab the back of her hair and yank her to the ground. Lying on her stomach, she winced in pain as strong hands pinned her body to the lawn. Jana cried out for help. Then she heard a familiar voice above her.

"Why couldn't you leave this alone?"

Tasting the grass beneath her lips, Jana cried, "Two people were murdered!"

"Two *blackmailers* were murdered, and they deserved to die. I tried to warn you. I threw a branch at you, pushed you...twice, wrote notes to you, killed your horse...hoping you would stop snooping. But you didn't. Now I'm forced to kill you, too!"

Smelling the familiar scent of her attacker on top of her, Jana's stomach pressed against the ground as she tried desperately to suck in life rendering air. The dark night grew darker before her eyes as Jana thought of her children and Brian.

I can't let this maniac take me away from my family.

Jana recalled a move she learned from the fight coordinator on *The Girl Detective*. She leaned forward and bent her elbows toward her attacker's forearm then slipped her wrist out of the hold. Next, Jana hooked onto her attacker's wrist with one hand and used her other hand to grasp behind the attacker's elbow, trapping the attacker's arm to Jana's chest. Finally, Jana kicked her attacker's knee then lifted her hips and turned over onto her knees. Once on top, Jana pressed the base of her palm into her attacker's nose and pushed with all her might until her attacker screamed in pain.

Jason cried, "Jana!"

"Jason!"

He ran out of the cottage and was at Jana's side in a flash. After helping Jana to her feet, he stood between Jana and her attacker.

Sitting on the lawn, Myrna Buller wiped the blood from her nose with the sleeve of her sequined gold sweatshirt. The former Olympiad said, "I warned you this would happen, Jason! Why didn't you listen to me?"

After making sure Jana was all right, Jason kneeled next to Myrna. "How could you do this?"

Myrna wept into his chest then looked up at him. "I did it for you, Jason. Everything has always been for *you*." Tears streamed down Myrna's cheeks. They mixed with the blood to create a pink waterfall flowing onto her sequined silver stretch pants. "I fell in love with you the first moment I laid eyes on you in that dreadful high school play in that hick town. There was something about you. A warmth, a sincerity, a lost child quality. And after I brought you to LA, we were a great team. You needed me, and I needed you."

"Myrna, you've done so much for me. Everything was going so well. Why did you have to ruin everything?"

Pointing at Jana, Myrna shouted, "*She* was going to ruin everything…by investigating your past. Just like Ryan O'Halloran, and that so-called reverend." She threw her arms around his strong back. "If the truth got out, it would have ended your career. The career *I* made…for *you*…for *us*." She released him and touched his cheek. "You are my vision of perfection." Myrna kissed him on the lips. "I'll always love you, Jason. I'll forever adore the flawless man I created."

Lieutenant Rivera and two police officers appeared next to Myrna.

Myrna looked at Jason in shock. "You called the police?"

Tears filled Jason's eyes. "I had to Myrna. I suspected, but I couldn't believe it was you doing all those things. When I saw you with Jana…I couldn't let you kill her, too."

As the police officers helped Myrna to her feet, she yelled, "You are *my* invention, Jason. You'll never belong to anyone else. You are mine…forever. I'll always love you, Jason, always!"

Lieutenant Rivera picked up Myrna's tortoise shell eyeglasses from the ground. "Are you all right, Mrs. Otley."

"I am now."

"You can both make your official statements tomorrow morning at the station."

Jason replied, "We'll be there."

Rivera scratched at his raven hair, covering the lawn around him with white. "Mrs. Otley, it appears I was wrong again about your instincts."

"Remember that for next time," she replied.

He cocked his head. "Will there be a next time?"

She smiled. "We'll see."

Rivera offered Jana a tiny bow then followed the police officers.

Being escorted away, Myrna said to the officers, "Don't squeeze my arms, bubalas. I'm a very important manager. I handle Jason Apollo, America's heartthrob. I discovered him. He's the biggest box office male star." She added proudly, "And he always will be."

Jason watched Myrna and the police officers disappear into the dark night. After wiping the tears off his face with the back of his hand, he put his arm around Jana and led her inside the guest cottage.

Minutes later, Jana sat on the brown suede couch next to a low burning fire in the brick fireplace. Jason draped a towel around her shoulders, as she rubbed her sore wrists.

Jason said, "Are you sure you're all right?"

"I'll be better if you tell me everything...from the beginning," she replied.

"I think you know most of it."

"I'd like to hear it from you."

Sitting next to her, Jason stared into the fire, reliving his past. "As you know, my childhood was pretty horrible. I didn't fit in anywhere. I was teased at school, shunned in the neighborhood, and misunderstood by my parents. I felt so alone...so completely isolated from everyone...including myself."

Jana said softly, "Until your senior play."

The fire reflected in Jason's clear blue eyes. "Being cast as Romeo opened up a new world for me. It helped me to find myself."

"And luck had it Myrna Buller saw a performance."

"Grace, who played Juliet, mentioned her mother's cousin was coming to see one of our shows. I had heard of Myrna Buller from her gymnastic days, but I didn't realize she had become a theatrical manager. You could have knocked me over with a feather after the performance. Not only because I was so skinny, but because the audience liked my performance."

"And Myrna Buller liked your performance."

"And she offered me a ticket out of Lynch, Kentucky."

"Weren't your parents concerned about you leaving Kentucky for Hollywood?"

"What could they do? I was turning eighteen and determined to go."

Jana faced him. "With Myrna...who saw you for who you really were?"

He nodded. "And for who *she* wanted me to be. In exchange for me signing an exclusive contract with her, Myrna paid for my personal trainer, acting, voice, and movement lessons, hair and clothing stylist, reconstructive facial surgery—"

"And your hormone injections and sexual reassignment surgery."

Jason ran a hand through his thick blond hair. "And Janice Appleton from Willow All Girls High School in Lynch, Kentucky became Jason Apollo from Cleveland, Ohio." He rose and stoked the fire. "After Myrna and I returned from Sweden, for the first time in my life I felt comfortable in my own skin. It was as if Myrna played God, correcting what always should have been. The man who was always inside me was finally able to show himself without mockery and disdain from others." He smiled. "And people noticed. Men admired me. Women threw themselves at my feet."

"Including Myrna?"

He rejoined Jana on the couch. "Myrna and I became fast friends. I was incredibly grateful for her belief in me...in the *real* me and for her generosity. As I grew older, Myrna wanted more, but she always understood that wasn't going to happen. Myrna was content to be my friend, confidant, and advisor. And thanks to her, my career took off, and eventually it soared. All went very well."

"Until you worked with Ryan O'Halloran on a film set. You two became friends, and you trusted him with the information that you were born in Lynch, Kentucky not Cleveland, Ohio, as you trusted with me."

Jason's muscles rippled underneath his sweatshirt and jeans. "They had technical issues on the film so we had long breaks. Ryan and I talked about our childhoods. He said his father was a ship builder who got cancer from working with asbestos. I told Ryan my father was a coal miner. He probed me about it, and I talked about the low wages and health hazards from environmental issues." He sighed. "When he asked me, without thinking, I told him my father's name was Frank Appleton."

"And once in Lynch to do his documentary, Ryan talked to your father and asked him questions, not only about coal mining, but also about *you*."

Jason nodded. "At first Dad didn't say much, but Ryan had a way of pulling a worm out of a bottle."

Jana rested her hand on his knee. "And Ryan tried

to blackmail Myrna in my study, wanting a package deal for him to direct a studio feature film in exchange for keeping your past a secret."

Jason rested his handsome face in his thick hands. "He wanted more than that. Ryan demanded Myrna place his name as director in every package she creates and never work with Jack Capello again. She told him the studios wouldn't finance an inexperienced director like him for big projects. But Ryan persisted, threatening to out me to the press as transgendered if Myrna didn't comply with his demand."

Ryan also blackmailed Tom and Trevor, Myrna's other clients, agreeing not to reveal their secrets in exchange for financing to edit and release his documentary. "So when no one was looking, Myrna pushed the light pole in the study that killed Ryan. And she also killed Reverend Charlton."

Jason looked at the wool rug. "When Gloria told Charlton what Ryan did to her, Charlton called Ryan onto the carpet, literally, in your hallway during our shoot in the study. Charlton demanded Ryan give him private information about others in the production company, or Charlton would go to the press about what Ryan did to Gloria."

And no doubt what Ryan did to Brenda Sue. Sliding to the edge of her seat, Jana said, "So Ryan named names, including *yours*."

Jason nodded. "Charlton tried to blackmail Myrna for a million dollars, knowing if the truth about Janice Appleton was leaked to the press, my career as America's male heartthrob would be finished."

"And when I asked questions about the murders, Myrna threw the branch at me, pushed me at my pool and in the woods, destroyed my doll, left me the two threatening notes, and killed Ginger."

He took her hands. "Jana, knowing about Ryan's and Charlton's blackmailing schemes, it was always in the back of my mind that it could be Myrna, but I never thought she was capable of doing those things."

Her blue eyes widened. "Will Myrna tell Lieutenant Rivera the truth about your past?"

Jason shook his head no. "Myrna would take the electric chair before doing that."

Throwing up her hands, she said, "When we talked about the murders, why didn't you tell me about Ryan and Charlton blackmailing Myrna?"

Jason looked like a lost little boy. "I thought you might not want to be with me…if you knew about my past."

She squeezed his hands. "Jason, dishonesty isn't a very good basis for a relationship." She smiled. "Especially when one of the two people is happily married."

His chiseled face was aglow with adoration. "Are you sure you are *happily* married?"

"*Very* sure."

Jason unleashed his straight white teeth. "You always said I wasn't like most men. You were right."

She threw her arms around his strapping back. "You're a good man, Jason. Just not the right man for me."

"So you aren't freaked out about my past?"

"If you can be friends with someone who was the peppy orphan, girl detective, school spy, and young mermaid, I can be friends with you."

"It's a deal." He gave her a bear hug.

A half hour later, Jana entered her mansion by the rear French doors into the kitchen. She heard voices coming from the great room, so she walked in that direction.

"Jana has been such an amazing role model for me. I hope I didn't freak her out too much trying to be like her. She's been like a mother to me. And speaking of mothers. When I finally convinced my mother to sit down and talk, she understood about Ryan O'Halloran. You and Jana are the perfect couple. I hope one day Trevor and I will be as happy as you two."

Stepping into the great room, Jana saw Gloria and Brian standing at the bar with Brian's suitcase at his feet.

"Brian!" Jana threw her arms around her husband.

He smothered her with kisses. "I missed you so much, babe."

"I missed you, too!" Tears streamed down Jana's cheeks as she buried her face in Brian's warm and welcoming chest.

Gloria smiled and went upstairs to check on Brian Jr.

The bar radio played "Hard to Say I'm Sorry" by Chicago.

Brian lifted Jana's face up to his. "I tried calling you all day to tell you my job is finished. Did you have a busy day?"

Throwing her arms around her husband's wide back, she said into his neck, "You could say that."

He took her in his arms. "I love you so much, babe."

"I love you, Brian." They shared a tender kiss which lasted into the night.

Epilogue

1983

Six months later, Jana and Brian rode in a white stretch limousine. Dressed in a low-cut red velvet gown with a ruby necklace, Jana clasped her hand through her husband's arm and squeezed. Wearing a black tuxedo with his chestnut hair slicked back in waves around his handsome face, Brian looked down at his wife and they shared a kiss.

Sitting opposite them was Trevor Masquer in a black leather tuxedo, and his fiancée, Gloria Covetry, wearing a daisy-colored taffeta gown. With his arm around Gloria, Trevor said, "Jana, I hope you understand about the way I acted during our film shoot. I'm a total method actor, so I was playing my role the entire time. I'm really nothing like that."

Gloria kissed Trevor's cheek. "He's a complete sweety, Jana. I adore this guy. So does my mother!"

He's all yours.

Trevor kissed Gloria's nose. "Gloria's coming with me on my next film shoot—to Africa. I play a young scientist who lives with a family of apes."

The apes will love you.

Sitting next to Jana, Simon Huckby adjusted the diaper underneath his swirled venetian-red and maize jumpsuit. "I've got a good offer for your next film,

245

baby doll."

"I hope it's not a Myrna Buller package deal," Brian said.

"Myrna's in jail where she belongs." Simon adjusted the scarlet beret on his bald head. "That'll teach her to mess with my baby girl."

Next to Simon, crouching down to fit inside the limousine, Cornelius Chamberlain adjusted his blue suspenders and bowtie. "I love it when you talk tough."

Simon and Cornelius shared a kiss.

The limousine pulled up in front of the Dorothy Chandler Pavilion in Hollywood.

As they stepped out of the limousine, Jana's face lit up as Tom Strong appeared at her side, on the arm of Hylas Summer. She kissed Tom's sunken cheek. "Tom, it's so good to see you."

"Right back at you," Tom replied, wearing a sagging tuxedo.

Hylas, in a leopard tuxedo and matching hat, said, "Jana, can you believe I finally hooked this gorgeous man?"

She kissed Hylas' cheek. "Congratulations to you both."

As Jana, Trevor, and Tom approached the theatre, members of the press swarmed around them on the red carpet like flies at a luau.

A rail-thin older woman in a purple gown aimed her microphone at Jana. "How did it feel coming back to moviemaking after a twenty-year absence, Jana?"

Jana unveiled a radiant smile that matched the halo effect of her hairstyle. "Like coming home."

A young man who looked like a Ken doll waved his microphone like a magic wand. "And that's exactly what it was like for you, Jana. How did you survive having the film shot on your own property?"

Jana giggled. "I didn't have a long commute to work."

The woman said, "Jana, you were America's little sweetheart. Though a real nail-biter, *His Obsession* is a bit...spicy. Will fans of your old movies accept the *new* Jana Lane?"

Jana replied, "The new Jana Lane isn't much different from the old one. She's just grown up."

Brian added, "I'm her husband, and I'm glad she *did*."

The female reporter laughed then said, "Jana, you've become an activist against AIDS. How would you respond to people who don't like that?"

Jana replied, "I'd tell them I'm going to keep up the fight until there is a cure."

Anxious to change the subject, the Ken doll said, "Trevor, congratulations on your nomination for Best Supporting Actor in *His Obsession*. How does it feel to be nominated at such a young age?"

Trevor said to the camera, "I studied my craft long and hard. Unlike some young stars, I didn't have family connections paving the way for me. I acted in regional theatre and came up the ladder the hard way. So I was totally prepared to take on this role, and I enjoyed every minute. I am honored to be nominated."

The woman in purple asked, "Tom, many of us were distraught to read you are retiring from acting. Please say it isn't so."

"I'm afraid it is." Tom added with a tear in his bloodshot eyes, "But how fortunate I was to shoot my last film with Jana Lane."

Jana squeezed his arm.

The woman turned to Jana. "Congratulations on your Academy Award nomination for Best Actress, Jana. It was an amazing performance and well deserved."

Simon said to the camera, "I'm Simon Huckby, Jana's agent. My baby doll is the greatest actress who ever lived. Always was. Always will be."

"No arguments there." Jason Apollo entered the red carpet, looking as handsome and strapping as ever in a white tuxedo with a white silk scarf around his neck. A famous young model was on his arm.

Jana offered Jason a hug, which he gratefully accepted and returned.

The female reporter smirked. "Jason, is it true you and Jana were an item during the filming of *His Obsession*?"

Jason replied, "Don't I wish? Unfortunately for me, Jana Lane is happily married to this lucky man."

Brian nodded to Jason.

"But Jana will always hold a special place in my heart," Jason added with a wink at Jana.

The Ken doll licked his lips like a dog at a butcher's convention. "Jason, your manager was imprisoned for double homicide during the shooting of this film. Do you keep in contact with her?"

Jason's handsome face turned solemn. "I call or visit Myrna every week. She is serving her time and seeing a therapist daily."

The female reporter pushed her partner away and eyed Jason's amazing physique. "Jason, we saw a great deal of you in *His Obsession*. Will we see even more of you in your next picture?"

Jason blushed. "My next picture is titled, *A Man's Man*, and I don't think my female fans will be disappointed."

Both reporters drooled.

Simon said, "My baby doll's next picture is called *Madam Senator*, and she will be terrific in it."

Jana's blue eyes sparkled. "Can you imagine *me* playing a senator in Washington, DC?"

Jason said, "If anyone can do it, Jana Lane can do it." He gazed at her. "Jana Lane can do *anything*."

After squeezing Jason's hand, Jana Lane Otley took her husband's arm and walked into the theatre.

A word about the author...

Joe Cosentino is the author of:
Paper Doll, the first Jana Lane mystery
Porcelain Doll, the second Jana Lane mystery
Drama Queen, the first Nicky and Noah mystery
An Infatuation
A Shooting Star
A Home for the Holidays
The Naked Prince and Other Tales from Fairyland,
The Nutcracker and the Mouse King.

As an actor he has appeared in principal roles in film, television, and theatre, opposite stars such as Bruce Willis, Rosie O'Donnell, Nathan Lane, Holland Taylor, Charles Keating, and Jason Robards.

His one-act plays, *Infatuation* and *Neighbor*, were performed in New York City. He wrote *The Perils of Pauline*, an educational film.

Joe is currently Head of the Department/Professor at a college in upstate New York, and is happily married. His upcoming novels are *Satin Doll* and *China Doll*, the third and fourth Jana Lane mysteries, and *Drama Muscle* and *Drama Cruise*, the second and third Nicky and Noah mysteries.

http://www.JoeCosentino.weebly.com